A Haunted Murder

A LIN COFFIN

COZY MYSTERY

BOOK 1

J.A. WHITING

To hear about new books and book sales, please sign up for my mailing list at: www.jawhitingbooks.com

For the loved ones who watch over us

CHAPTER 1 – TWENTY YEARS AGO

Carolin Coffin was never afraid of the dark. Not the way other kids were. Before she could even talk she was able to see things that "normal" kids couldn't. The spirits of people who had passed never scared her. Whenever a spirit appeared, she always felt a sense of benevolence and calm.

She didn't like calling them ghosts, but that was the easiest way to think of them. Sometimes the ghosts would speak to her mind, but mostly they were quiet.

Lin figured out pretty early that other people couldn't see what she could, so she stopped allowing the spirits to reveal themselves. When they were coming, she could feel the hairs on her arms stand up or a coolness brush past her.

She didn't want to be different or made fun of, so she turned away from what she could see and hear. When she felt a ghost approaching, she would push down inside herself and think of cotton balls all around her, or a cloud or some magic fog surrounding her that nothing could get through.

1

After a while, the spirits stopped coming and she was more like the other kids her age. The last time she saw a spirit was at a neighborhood summer party when she was nine years old.

All the kids had a get-together in one of the neighborhood girl's backyards. There was a cookout and games and when the sun went down, the girl's parents made a campfire for toasting marshmallows and everyone sat around it in the dark swatting at mosquitoes.

Some kids started telling ghost stories and murder stories and a few of the younger kids started to cry and ran inside to tell on the ones who were making up the scary tales. The kids who were telling the tales ran inside to defend themselves.

Lin stayed by the fire. She liked looking up at the stars and watching the flames dancing and making shadows against the trees. It was quiet and peaceful without all the fussing and crying and she hoped the others would stay inside for a while.

One other kid stayed outside, too. His name was Pete and he was about twelve years old. Pete had come up from New York City to stay with a family in the neighborhood for a few weeks. He was sponsored by a group called something like the Country Air Experience. Lin liked Pete. He had a self assurance and self acceptance that many kids lacked, that most adults lacked for that matter. He never got flustered and didn't seem to like drama and foolishness.

Pete looked across the fire at Lin. "Why aren't you scared of the stories?"

She shrugged. "What's to be scared of?"

"The other kids are scared."

Lin made eye contact with Pete. "You're not."

He shook his head.

"Why not?" Lin asked.

"Real life stuff is the stuff to be afraid of. Not made up stories."

"What are you afraid of?" Lin cocked her head.

"People. Some people. And the stuff they do." Pete paused. "What are you afraid of?"

Lin didn't give him an answer, she just poked the toe of her sneaker around in the dirt.

They were both quiet for a minute, and then Pete asked, "Being different?"

Lin's head jerked up and she could feel her cheeks warm. She was glad that it was dark so he couldn't see the fluster on her face. "What?"

"Being different, being alone. You want to fit in," Pete said. "But it's better to be yourself."

Before Lin could think of a reply, the hairs on her arms stood at attention and a cool shiver rolled over her skin. Atoms began to swirl and sparkle, and then a small woman with a pleasant smile materialized standing two feet away from Pete. The woman's essence shimmered and her body was translucent. The spirit gazed at Pete with a gentle look on her face, and then she turned to Lin.

Lin smiled. Pete looked just like the woman.

Pete turned his head. "What are you staring at?"

Lin's eyes met his. She wasn't going to say anything, but then the kind ghost woman spoke to her mind and Lin had to reveal the words.

She took a deep breath. "You mom wants you to know that she's okay. She's proud of you, Pete. She said 'let go of it and be the man you are meant to become.'"

Pete's eyes grew wide and his mouth dropped open. His head turned to his right and then back to Lin. "What did you say?" His voice was high and squeaky.

"You look just like her," Lin said softly. "Your mom."

A figure stepped from the wooded property line. The ghost woman disappeared into the night air like wisps of smoke from the fire. Pete and Lin both turned to the girl who had emerged from behind a tree.

"I heard you, Lin. You're a freak," she spat.

It was Lin's nine-year-old neighbor, Charlene Sheldon. They used to be good friends until Lin made the mistake of telling her about the things she could see.

"You tell lies just to seem special." Charlene had her hands on her hips. "I'm going to tell." Her voice was haughty.

Anger boiled inside of Lin mostly because Charlene had spoiled the moment and made the ghost go away, but also because she was sick of

Charlene putting her down and telling the other kids she was a freak. A resolve hardened in Lin's chest.

Mrs. Sheldon came out of the back door of the house and called across the darkness. "You other kids. Come on in here now. The party's over. Everybody's going home. Come on."

Charlene yelled to her mother. "Lin's telling lies again."

"Come in here. No more stories," Mrs. Sheldon said. "It's time to go."

Charlene didn't budge, but Lin stood up, dusted off her butt, and strode across the lawn to the house like she didn't care about Charlene or anybody else. She did though, she cared a lot. Lin hurried to the back door, blinking hard to keep her tears from falling.

"Lin," Pete called. He trotted up beside her. "Lin."

Lin looked at him out of the corner of her eye, expecting some rude comment. She kept walking.

Pete touched her arm. "Thanks," he whispered.

Lin turned slightly. She gave Pete a little nod.

Mrs. Sheldon eyed the young girl as if she was frightened by her, but the woman didn't say a word as Lin went into the house to wait for her grandpa to come and pick her up.

The nine-year-old sat down heavily in one of the kitchen chairs. She was so tired of people giving her weird looks and saying mean things to her.

A few months later, Grandpa and Lin left the suburbs for good. They moved to Cambridge, Massachusetts where she made a new start as a 'normal' kid.

That night at the Sheldon's party was the last time Carolin Coffin allowed herself to see what other people couldn't.

CHAPTER 2 – PRESENT DAY

The fast-ferry let out three, long, low blares as it approached the dock in Nantucket town. The ride had taken just under an hour to cross Nantucket Sound from Hyannis, Massachusetts. For the last few minutes of the ride, Lin stood aft on the open deck, the wind pummeling her long brown hair into a cloud that whipped all around her head. Her dog, a small light brown mixed breed with a darker patch of brown on his right eye, watched his owner through the glass window of the door from inside the passenger cabin.

Lin opened the door. She reached for her rolling suitcase and swung her small duffle bag over her shoulder. "Come on, Nick. Let's go find Viv."

The dog wagged his little stub of a tail and they joined the line of disembarking passengers. Walking down the stairs to the dock, Lin admired the bright blue of the sky. It was a perfect early June day, with warm temperatures and a light, comfortable breeze. Tourists strolled along the brick walkways browsing the shops and a crowd of people gathered on the sidewalk to greet relatives and friends as they descended from the gangplank.

A short, pretty young woman caught Lin's eye. She waved with vigor from under a shade tree. Vivian Coffin and Lin were cousins who shared the same birthday and had just turned twenty-nine. Viv had lived on Nantucket all of her life except for her four years away at college and a summer spent in Europe traveling with a choral group. The girls were descended from two different lines of the Coffin family on their fathers' sides, but their mothers had been sisters whose ancestors were from the Witchard family of Nantucket.

"Carolin!" Viv called to her cousin, her blue eyes shining. Lin preferred to be called "Lin" but sometimes Viv referred to her by her formal name.

Viv hurried forward. She carried a few extra pounds, had chin-length light brown hair flecked with gold. It was cut in layers around her face. Her perfect skin was complemented by rosy cheeks and a warm, lovely smile.

Lin wrapped her cousin in a big hug while Nicky danced around expecting attention.

Viv reached into her pocket and withdrew a dog biscuit. Nicky sat down and looked eagerly at Viv, but he politely waited for the treat. Viv bent to pat the dog. "How's Tricky Nicky?" She scratched his head and handed him the biscuit.

Taking the duffel bag from her cousin, Viv slipped her arm through Lin's. "I'm so glad you're here. It's going to be so much fun with you on the island."

Walking with her cousin over the cobblestone streets of the quaint town made Lin's heart swell with happiness and she could feel all of the stress of the past months slip from her shoulders and fall away. *Well, almost all.* The past six months had been the hardest time of her life, with the sudden death of her grandfather and the discovery that her long-time boyfriend had been cheating on her. The combination of events nearly broke her heart. Lin had been feeling alone and adrift and she hoped that moving to the island would be a new start.

"I went by the cottage again yesterday." Viv had been keeping an eye on the cottage that Lin had inherited from her grandfather. "Everything looks good. I put some food in your refrigerator to tide you over until you get to the market. The truck is going okay, but it won't last forever." Off and on, over the past few months, Viv had been driving the old truck that had come with the cottage to keep it in running order. "I took it in for service. I think it will make it through the summer so you can use it for your gardening business, but you'll have to replace it after that."

Lin thanked Viv for all of her help. After inheriting the cottage, Lin saw an online ad advertising a gardening business for sale on Nantucket. She contacted the woman and they closed a deal. The work consisted mainly of driving around to client's homes on the island and taking care of their gardens and window boxes in addition to some lawn mowing and trimming.

The girls stopped on the sidewalk in front of Viv's bookstore and café, *Viv's Victus*. Viv sold paperbacks, hardcovers, and audiobooks, and in the small café in the back corner of the store, she served beverages, soups, sandwiches, salads, and sweet treats. Most evenings in the summer, musical groups performed in the café and Viv's band played there on Tuesday and Thursday nights.

"How's business?" Lin asked.

"It's okay. The off-season is slow, but we're coming into the busiest few months of the year, so I'm optimistic."

The cousins parted ways after arranging to meet for dinner later in the evening. Lin was eager to get to the cottage and unpack and Viv needed to return to work.

With his owner hurrying after him, Nicky led the way up Main Street along the brick sidewalks lined with shade trees. Lin loved the old houses and mansions that lined the street. In the late 1700s, the island had been home to sixty percent of the New England whaling fleet. Considered one the finest surviving examples of a late 18th- and early 19th century New England seaport, the entire island had been designated a National Historic district.

The dog turned left when he reached the memorial in the small traffic rotary.

"You remember the way?" Lin marveled at the dog's memory. They hadn't been on-island for over six months. She waited to see if Nicky would take the turn onto Vestry Road and she laughed out loud and shook her head in amazement when the dog sauntered along onto the correct side street.

The girl and dog passed small and medium sized homes sided with weathered silver-gray shingles. Many of the homes had crushed white shell driveways, flowers spilling from gardens and window boxes, and roses climbing over white picket fences.

As they approached their cottage, Lin let out a contented sigh. She had so many happy memories of the wonderful summers spent at the house with her grandfather. Nicky gave a bark and danced around the front stoop while the young woman pulled out the key, opened the door, and stepped into the little entryway of their new home.

Thanks, Grandpa. Tears of gratitude gathered in Lin's eyes.

***

Nicky napped on the floor in the living room in a pool of sunshine while Lin biked to the market. The dog perked up when his owner returned and he watched her put away the groceries. The house was arranged in the shape of a "U" with a deck in the middle built between the three sides. A huge kitchen with a center island and an old wooden dining table took up most of the left section of the house. Off the kitchen, there was a laundry room and a full bath.

On the other side, Grandpa had built a master bedroom and bath and the center of the cottage housed a good-sized living room with huge windows and a door leading out to the deck. An unfinished second floor had space for additional bedrooms and a sitting area, but Lin had more than enough space in the first floor layout.

There was a small second bedroom next to the master that Lin planned to use as her office. Before coming to the island, she'd worked as a computer programmer for a small start-up company in Cambridge and, not wanting to lose such a talented employee, the business worked out an arrangement so that she could work part-time remotely from Nantucket.

Lin went around opening windows to let in fresh air. Bustling about the cottage, she put clothes away, dusted all the surfaces, and swept the wood floors in each of the rooms. She made her bed with pale blue linens that had navy blue anchors printed on the fabric. Taking two soft blankets from the closet, Lin folded them, placed one in a corner of the living room and the other on the floor near her bed. She looked at the dog. "You have these to sleep on until we can get to the store for proper dog beds."

Nicky let out a tiny woof, tested the blanket in the living room with his two front paws, and giving it the seal of approval, turned in three circles and settled down. Lin made some tea and wandered over to the wall of bookshelves where she removed two volumes, one on the gardens of Nantucket and the other about haunted houses on the island. Lin loved crossword puzzles and anagram puzzles and she pulled some out of her bag. She carried the books and puzzles to a comfy easy chair placed next to the gas stove and she sank onto the cushion. After turning some pages of the garden book, her head rested against the back of the chair, and in two minutes, she was sound asleep.

***

Lin jerked awake from a small brown head pushing against her leg. She rubbed her eyes and looked about the room, disoriented. Nicky put his paws on her chair and gave a whine to indicate it was time to be let outside. Lin pushed herself up and took a quick look at the wall clock, afraid she was late to meet Viv for dinner. She let out a sigh of relief when she realized that she still had an hour before she was supposed to be at the restaurant.

Lin and the dog stepped onto the deck. Nicky ran off to the rear of the property while Lin stepped down from the deck onto the stone patio that ran the length of the house. A short stone wall stood along the edge of the patio and beyond was a bit of lawn ringed by bushes and trees.

The sun had sunk behind the wooded property line. Lin stretched and yawned and turned her attention to the field behind the neighbor's house. A strange mist rose from the land and hung in the air several feet above the grasses. Part of the fog rode the breeze and floated into Lin's backyard. Admiring the way the mist softened the landscape, she pulled her phone from her pocket to photograph the mysterious looking scene.

She took two shots and brought one of the photos into view on the phone screen. Smiling at how nice it came out, she used her fingers to enlarge the first photograph. A gasp escaped from Lin's throat and her eyes bugged from their sockets. Her hand shook so violently from what she saw on the phone's screen that it slipped from her hand and she had to move like a juggler to keep from dropping it.

An icy chill raced through her inner core. She looked at the photo on the screen again. There in the mist of her backyard, stood an old man dressed in eighteenth-century style clothing. His hair was gray and the sides hung down and touched the top of his shirt collar. Lin's head jerked around to the wooded area behind the house, her eyes searching for the man.

No one was there. She looked back at the phone and used her finger to swipe to the second photograph. It was a lovely shot of the misty landscape. She swiped back to the first picture. Enlarging it, she brought the phone close to her eyes.

The man was no longer in the shot. Lin blinked hard several times and switched back and forth between the two photos.

Her heart pounding, she turned again to look out over her yard and the adjacent field. The mist was clearing, rising up and evaporating. She jumped when Nicky pressed his cool nose against her leg.

"I didn't see you come back." Lin's heart was still racing as she reached down to pat the dog's head. Glancing back over her shoulder, she headed for the door to the living room. "Come on, Nick. Let's go inside."

As she reached for the doorknob, the brown dog woofed. Lin looked down at him. He was gazing towards the field, wagging his tail, and whining. Scanning the field one more time, her hand shook as she turned away, grasped the knob, and opened the door. "Come, Nick. I need to go meet Viv." Her voice was shaky.

Reluctantly, the little dog entered the living room with his owner. Lin closed the door and bolted the lock. She wondered how in the world she could have imagined that there had been a man in her photograph.

CHAPTER 3

Lin walked through town dodging the tourists who strolled past the shops and restaurants. She headed to one of the popular pubs down near the boat docks where many locals hung out enjoying tasty food and a drink or two.

Lin spotted her cousin standing near the entrance to the pub. Viv was talking to a man who looked to be in his forties. The man was tall and thin. He had a dark tan and his salt and pepper colored hair was cut close to his scalp. He looked like someone who spent many hours outdoors in the sun.

Lines creased Viv's forehead giving her a serious expression and her shoulders were pulled straight up in an almost defensive posture. Her lips were tight as she shook her head. Clearly the two people were engaged in a heated discussion, but Lin couldn't imagine what was causing Viv's annoyance. A surge of adrenaline pulsed through Lin's body.

"You need to stop asking me." Viv's hand flew

about like a bird evading capture. "I've told you over and over, I have no interest whatsoever."

The man took a menacing step closer.

Lin approached and stood next to her cousin. "What's going on?" She glanced at Viv before turning her attention to the man. "Is there a problem?"

"Yeah, there's a problem." The man's dark eyes flashed at Lin. "You might want to stay out of it."

"And you might want to mind your manners." Lin had a hand on her hip. "We're late to meet our friends. Have a nice evening." She looped her arm around Viv's waist and led her away from the harassing pest. Lowering her voice, she asked, "Who is that? What's he going on about?"

Viv exhaled loudly and rolled her eyes. "He has been haunting me the past couple of weeks. He shows up at the bookstore, he stands on the sidewalk outside my house. I walk around in town doing errands and I spot him watching me."

"He asks you out?"

"God, no." Viv shook her head. "He wants to buy my house."

Lin's eyes went wide. "He follows you around like some creep because he wants to buy your house?"

"It's weird, isn't it?"

Since their friends hadn't arrived yet, the hostess showed them to a table.

Lin was concerned. "Did you report him to the

police?"

Viv held her hands up. "What would I say to them? I see a man around town. Sometimes he comes into my bookstore?"

"Tell them he's a creep who keeps bothering you."

Viv tilted her head to one side. "It would just make me seem like the crazy one."

Lin sighed. "I guess. Maybe you should file a report anyway, just to have it on record."

The waitress brought glasses of water and Viv lifted hers to her lips and gulped. She ordered a beer that was brewed on the island and Lin ordered a glass of sangria.

"When did that guy first show up?" Lin leaned in closer. "He made you an offer for your house? Is he from the island?"

A smile spread over Viv's lips. "I don't need to go to the police since I have an interrogator right here." She chuckled. "He knocked on my door one evening. He introduced himself and said he would be very interested in purchasing my property because he'd always admired it." Viv crossed her arms and leaned on the table. "I thanked him, but said I'd grown up in the house and that I was planning to remain there until I grew old."

"What did he say to that?" Lin worried that this man might be using the desire to buy the house to disguise other intentions.

"He said that maybe I'd like to hear his offer. I

told him it wouldn't make any difference and thanked him again. I suggested he go talk to John so that he could find an appropriate home for him." Viv's boyfriend of six years, John Clayton, was an island Realtor. He lived on a boat in the harbor and was also a musician who played several instruments. He and Viv had been playing together in bands for years.

Viv continued. "The guy became disgruntled. His reaction made me nervous so I said I was expecting visitors and had to see to something I had in the oven."

"Did he go away?"

Viv ran her hand threw her hair. "He told me that he would speak to me another time. Then he left."

"He showed up again?"

"Many times. At the bookstore, knocking on my door at the house. I'd see him at the market and he'd start again with his offers. He always made it seem like we'd just run into each other by accident, but I think he was following me around."

"Why is he so adamant about buying your house?" Lin was thinking out loud. "Is he from the island?"

"I tried to get information from him about why he was so interested in this particular house, but he wasn't very forthcoming. I asked a few people about him and I looked him up on the internet. His name is Greg Hammond. He runs a large landscape design business, does a lot of patios, walkways, stone walls, things like that, in addition to landscaping with plants. He's got a house and a big barn and greenhouse out towards 'Sconset way."

"Your house wouldn't fit his needs if he's a running a business like that."

"He says that he's keeping his present property. He wants my house, too." Viv frowned. "But why? Is he crazy or is there some legitimate reason to want it so badly?"

"We should look up his background. Maybe discreetly talk to some of his employees or customers. I could approach someone he's done work for and tell them I was thinking of hiring him and ask how things went with him."

Viv nodded. She seemed to be thinking something over. She made eye contact with her cousin and lowered her voice. "I keep thinking there must be something in particular about *my* house. Its history? Its design and layout? I don't know."

Lin smiled. "Maybe there's a huge oil deposit under the house. He'll tap into it and make millions."

That comment elicited a loud chuckle from Viv. Her big blue eyes sparkled. She was just about to say something else when her boyfriend, John, and her assistant manager from the bookstore, Mallory, walked into the restaurant at the same time and hurried over. John gave Viv a kiss and then he greeted Lin with a hug. Mallory and Lin had met a few times. The two women greeted each other warmly.

The waitress returned and took drink orders from the two newcomers.

Mallory looked across the table at Viv. "Guess who I saw storming up the street just now?"

Viv made a face. "Let me guess. Was it Mr. Crazy House?" Viv, John, and Mallory had christened Greg Hammond with the more descriptive name. "He spoke with me just a few minutes ago, or should I say 'argued?'"

"Ugh. That guy won't give up." Mallory shook her head. She couldn't believe that Hammond had spoken with Viv twice in the same day. "He seems to be getting more desperate."

John's eyes narrowed and his lips turned down. "This worries me." He put his arm protectively around his girlfriend's shoulders. "I don't like it. Why don't we go to the police station tomorrow? I think it's a good idea to have a report of this man's harassment on record."

"My very words," Lin agreed.

Viv's eyes darkened. "Why can't he leave me alone?" She groaned. "I guess you're right. Let's go to the police station later in the afternoon though. I don't want to be away from the store in the morning. All the regulars come in for coffee and pastry. I like to be there then."

With that decided, the group dug into their meals and the talk turned to music and books and movies. Even though she was enjoying herself, Lin couldn't shake the feeling of unease that had settled in her chest because of Greg Hammond's pestering of Viv. Not only that, but she was still disturbed by her hallucination of the man in the back field appearing in her photograph.

When the girls had been in their early teens, Lin had shared with her cousin that she was able to see spirits. She braced hard for Viv's response, but Viv was excited by the news and wanted to hear all about it. She didn't think Lin was crazy or weird or a liar.

It was the first time that Lin could remember having felt valued and respected for who she was with someone other than her grandpa, and it made her feel that she could tell her cousin anything. Lin had planned to tell Viv about the photograph during dinner, but she didn't get the chance because of the talk about Greg Hammond and his quest for Viv's house.

A musical group set up in the corner of the restaurant and started to play Irish folksongs with a rock edge. After just a few bars of the first song, the clientele was clapping hands, stomping feet to the beat, and some were singing along. Lin and the others stayed until after midnight enjoying the company of the crowd and the upbeat music.

After calling it a night and saying goodbye to

everyone, Lin walked up Main Street under the streetlamps. As she headed for home, worry over Viv and the man in the photograph caused a heavy sense of dread to fall over her shoulders like a heavy, woolen, eighteenth-century cloak.

CHAPTER 4

Up early the next morning, Lin and Nicky strolled down Main Street into town. A soft breeze off the ocean kept the early morning air clear and comfortable. Lin planned to stop at Viv's bookstore/café for some tea and something to eat before heading off to open a bank account and arrange with the cable company to come to the house to install internet.

The brown dog wagged its tail at everyone they passed. The animal was under the impression that all humans, cats, and dogs were his friends, and he was shocked to discover on rare occasions that he was wrong.

When Lin arrived home last night from having dinner with Viv and the others, Nicky dragged himself off his blanket and met her, sleepy-eyed, at the door. She let him outside for a few minutes and then the two stumbled into the bedroom and fell asleep. Once Lin started her landscaping job, the small brown dog would join her on her rounds, but on evenings when she was out or had other things to do, she didn't like the poor creature to be stuck in the house so she'd arranged for a carpenter to come and give her an estimate on the installation of a doggy door.

When they reached the bookstore, the front door was open, a bowl of water was set out for any dogs passing by, and two huge pots of flowers stood to the side. The bookstore had dark wooden shelves stacked with paperbacks and hardcovers and several tables stood in the center aisle displaying bestsellers and books recommended and chosen by the staff. In the rear of the space was the café with a counter to place orders for drinks or treats. Several groups of comfortable sofas and chairs were placed near the counter area, and tables and chairs were clustered to one side. The cozy shop had tin ceilings and gleaming wood floors.

Viv's store was always crowded with customers reading on laptops and handheld devices, paging through books, and having a bite to eat or something to drink. Her dark gray cat perched on an easy chair observing the goings-on. Dogs were welcome in the store as long as they got along with the queen of the domain.

Nicky's tail wagged at the sight of the cat and he approached slowly. He rested his head on the easy chair with his snout only an inch from the lovely cat's paws. She watched him for a moment, and then placed one paw gently on the dog's nose.

"The queen has given her blessing." Viv came

around the corner of a bookshelf. "Do you think they remember meeting before?"

Lin scratched Queenie's cheeks and the cat purred. "I bet they remember each other."

Nicky jumped onto the easy chair and snuggled next to the cat. Queenie moved closer to the arm of the chair away from him, but she allowed the friendly animal to stay.

"Whoa." Viv's eyes bugged out watching the interaction between the cat and dog and she chuckled. "*That* is a first."

Lin shook her head at the dog's bold move as she walked to the counter to order tea and a cornbread muffin. "Any early morning visits from Mr. Crazy House?"

Viv rolled her eyes. "No, but the day is young." She gave a forced smile. "I got here late. I slept through the alarm because of our late dinner last night."

"It was hard to get out of bed," Lin agreed, and then she lowered her voice. "I want to tell you about something strange that happened to me at the house yesterday." She needed to tell her cousin about the episode with the photograph.

Viv gave her cousin a quizzical look. "Okay, grab something to drink. An employee called in sick and now I'm really running behind. Let me get some things done and in a few minutes I'll come and sit with you."

Lin carried her tea and muffin to a vacated table

and sat down. Viv bustled about behind the counter pouring teas and brewing coffees for her customers. A minute after Lin took her seat, an older woman spoke to her from one of the sofas.

"Aren't you Merry Witchard Coffin's daughter?"

Lin, surprised, shifted her blue eyes towards the voice. A slender older woman with short white hair feathered around her face sat with three friends in one of the clusters of comfortable furniture. The group had quieted and they were staring at Lin making her feel uncomfortably on display.

"Yes." Lin gave a slight nod. "I'm Merry's daughter."

"I knew your grandfather." The white-haired woman had piercing blue eyes and beautiful skin. "He was a member of our early-morning chat sessions." She gestured towards the people sitting with her. "We miss him."

Lin's eyes grew moist and she swallowed hard. "Me, too."

The four people gave their names, but Lin was so surprised to be noticed that she immediately forgot what they said. Later she would have to question Viv about who they were.

"Your name is Carolin?" One of the older men asked.

Lin nodded again.

"Your grandfather was mighty proud of you," the man said.

Lin blushed and smiled.

27

"Welcome, my dear." A second woman with pale blonde hair smiled. "You need anything? You just yell."

Lin's heart swelled and her throat felt tight. She managed a squeaky, "Thank you." She knew her grandfather had met most mornings with a group of friends for coffee, but she'd never met any of them. She was warmed by their heartfelt welcome.

"You're moving into your grandfather's place?" The second man questioned.

"I am. I just arrived yesterday afternoon and got a few things settled."

The blonde woman gave her a friendly smile. "You're planning on staying then?"

"I hope so. If everything works out."

The first man took a sip from his mug. "Will you be working here with Viv?"

Lin shook her head and told them about her part-time job as a software architect and about buying the small gardening business. "I like to be outside and can use the extra money, so I hope the two jobs will be enough."

The blonde said, "How wonderful to have another Coffin on the island." The comment sounded strange. Lin got plenty of teasing about her last name when she was growing up. People off-island had no idea about the long history of the Coffin family and their importance to Nantucket.

The white-haired woman smiled at Lin and held her eyes. "And it's wonderful to have another

Witchard with us, as well."

Lin took a sip of her tea and glanced over at Nicky and Queenie to be sure they were behaving. Queenie bolted up. She turned her amber-colored eyes to the front of the store and let out a low growl. Nicky sat up, sniffing the air.

A middle-aged man burst into the bookstore and hurried to the café section. His cheeks were flushed and he was out of breath. His entrance into the store was so sudden that the customers stopped what they were doing and turned to look at him.

Viv looked up from behind the counter and was about to greet the man, but hesitated when she noticed the look on his face. "Are you okay, Rob?"

The man's voice was breathless. "Someone's been killed. Down at the docks. There's been a murder."

Viv's eyes widened into saucers and she clutched the counter. Lin nearly toppled her chair as she ran to her cousin. Viv's boyfriend lived on his boat down in the harbor.

"I saw John this morning. It's not him." Viv reassured Lin, but she worried it might be one of her customers.

Several patrons rose from their seats to gather around the man who had brought the news. People fired questions at him.

"Who was it?"

"What happened?"

"Someone was murdered?"

"Is anyone in custody?"

Some people rushed out the front door of the bookstore to head down to the docks to get the information first-hand.

The white-haired woman who had first spoken to Lin stood up. "Who was killed?" Her voice held a tone of authority.

The bearer of the news wiped sweat from his brow. "It was that landscaper who had a boat down there. Greg Hammond."

Viv gasped. *Mr. Crazy House.* The room started to spin in her vision. Lin grabbed her arm just in time to ease her fall to the floor.

When her bottom hit hard against the wood, the jostling brought her out of her near-faint. "Oh, gosh." Viv put a hand to her forehead. "I got dizzy."

Lin knelt beside her. "Just breathe normally. The news surprised you. Sit for a minute. You'll feel better soon."

Some customers leaned over the serving counter to get a look at Viv to see if she was okay. One asked, "Should I call an ambulance?"

Viv flapped her hand in the air. "No, no. I'm okay."

Mallory brought a cool glass of water. "Can I get you anything else?"

Viv brought the glass to her lips and sipped. She held the side of the glass next to her temple. "I feel like a fool."

Nicky darted to Viv's side and gave her a lick on the face. Queenie watched the proceedings and when she was satisfied that her owner was unhurt, she sauntered back to her chair.

Viv looked at her cousin. "Would you go down to the docks and see what happened? Ask around? Find out what's being said." She leaned closer. "Does Hammond's murder have anything to do with my house?"

Lin's blue eyes went wide. She hadn't considered that possibility. Was Greg Hammond onto something about Viv's house? Was it something so important that a person would kill over it? Was her cousin in danger?

Viv pushed herself up off the floor with Mallory gripping an arm on one side and Lin on the other.

"You should sit for a while. Get your equilibrium back." Lin held Viv's arm and steered her to one of the café chairs.

"Will you go see what's going on at the docks?" Viv sat. "Come back and tell me?"

Lin glanced at Mallory who nodded. "I'll be here. I'll keep an eye on her. Go see what's happening down there."

Viv said, "And leave Nicky here. There will be too many people around. He'll get lost in the crowd."

Lin reluctantly left the bookstore. She would have preferred to stay to be sure Viv was okay, but she couldn't say no to Viv's request. She hurried down the streets for several blocks. A large crowd was gathered behind a police barrier. Access to the dock area was blocked. Lin moved close to the people who were standing and watching.

"What's happened? Someone was killed?" She pretended not to know much which wasn't hard since she really didn't know any details. She hoped that the man who'd brought the news was mistaken and that Greg Hammond had only suffered a cut or some other wound and was still alive.

A man turned to answer Lin's question. "Guy's name was Hammond. He's dead."

"Was it an accident?" Lin's blue eyes took in the scene of commotion. Blue lights flashed on the tops of police cars, official looking people hurried back and forth, and an ambulance was parked near the docks with its rear doors wide open.

"It was a murder," someone else from the crowd offered.

"Shot?" Although Lin felt ghoulish asking for specifics, she wanted to gather as much information as possible.

"Stabbed to death."

Lin's stomach lurched. She took some deep breaths and then moved along the edge of the crowd. She could see a man being questioned by one of the police officers and scooted as close to the barrier as she could manage.

"You said you saw someone near the boat this morning?" the officer asked.

An older fisherman with gray hair and a wiry build scratched his head. "Yup. It was early this morning. It was that girl who runs the bookstore. She was down here near Hammond's boat. I saw her run away."

Lin suppressed a gasp as a cold shiver ran down her back. *Why was Viv near Hammond's boat this morning? Why did she run away?"*

CHAPTER 5

Lin's heart was hammering double-time. She strained to hear what more the fisherman was telling the officer, but a couple of men next to her were loudly sharing opinions about the crime which hindered her ability to understand the fisherman's words. She watched as the police officer wrote something in a small notebook. The officer stepped away from the gray-haired fisherman and the guy turned and started to move down the docks away from Lin. She searched for a way to follow him, but the area was blocked off and only those who owned boats or had business near the docks were permitted to enter.

She lingered with the crowd for twenty more minutes listening to conversations. The same facts were being rehashed and nothing new surfaced. Lin could see the police questioning other people on the dock, but they were too far away to hear what was being said.

A sudden, chill breeze made goosebumps rise up on Lin's skin and she rubbed her arms with both hands before she realized that the air was warm and there was no breeze. Understanding what had caused the sensation made her breath catch in her throat and she froze, her fingers trembling. Narrowing her eyes, afraid of what she would see, Lin turned her head slowly towards the boat dock. Her chest tightened, sounds became muffled, and the movement around her seemed to slow.

A translucent figure stood on the dock next to Greg Hammond's boat, an old man, wearing eighteenth-century clothes. He made eye contact with Lin and her throat constricted.

The man from the photograph.

***

Lin whirled away, weaved through the cobbled streets, and jogged up Main Street to Viv's bookstore. Puffing, she stood on the sidewalk to catch her breath and collect herself. When she entered the store, she didn't want to appear as panicked as she felt.

The bookstore crowd had thinned considerably and now just a few people were sitting at café tables reading. Approaching the counter near the back wall of the store, Lin saw Nicky still perched next to Queenie on the upholstered chair. The cat gave Lin a knowing look. The dog jumped down to greet his owner, wiggling and wagging.

"Good boy." Lin patted the dog's head.

J.A Whiting

Viv's eyes were wide with worry. "What did you learn?" She came around from behind the counter. Viv could see the anxiety on her cousin's face. They took the table that was furthest away from the other customers. "What is it?"

Lin told her what she'd heard the fisherman say and Viv's face blanched.

She explained, "I went to the docks before coming to the bookstore to drop off some muffins to John. He had left for work already so I left them on his boat. I was running late. I decided to leave the docks by going out on the west end of the wharf so that I could cut through the back way to get to Main Street quicker." Her face lost more of its color. "When I was hurrying past some of the boats, I heard Greg Hammond's voice. I thought he was walking up behind me, but the voice was coming from inside his boat cabin." Viv's face muscles drooped.

"What happened? Did Hammond see you? Did he come after you?"

Viv shook her head. "I could hear angry voices. It sounded like two men arguing inside the cabin. I heard Greg shout, but I couldn't make out the words. I was afraid of him, Lin. My instinct was to get out of there. I broke into a run." She pressed her fingertips to her temple. "Maybe I should have called the police." Viv's wide eyes searched her cousin's face. "Is he dead because I ran away?"

Lin touched her cousin's arm. "Of course not.

36

You were just passing by. You didn't know what was going on. Hammond had been harassing you. It made sense to get away."

Viv blinked several times. Her bottom lip trembled. "I'm glad you're here."

The corners of Lin's mouth turned up. "I'm glad I'm here, too." She took a deep breath. "I think you should go tell the police what you heard this morning."

"Really?" Viv made a face.

Lin nodded. "You don't want them thinking you're a suspect. It's better to be forthcoming. Don't give them the idea that you're hiding anything." She gave an encouraging smile. "Maybe go now, before they get the idea to question you."

Viv's eyes shifted to the center aisle of the store and her face muscles tensed up. "Too late."

Lin turned to see a police officer headed their way.

***

The officer approached the girls' table. "Vivian Coffin?"

"That's me." Viv stood up. Her dark golden highlights glimmered in the soft light of the ceiling chandelier.

"A word, please?" The police officer's face was serious.

The gray cat arched her back and hissed at the

man in the blue uniform.

Viv gestured to Lin. "This is my cousin, Carolin Coffin. You can speak in front of her."

"In private, if you don't mind." The officer glanced around the space. "Is there somewhere we can go to talk? Do you have an office?"

Viv nodded. "It's this way." She gestured to the other side of the store.

As Lin watched them head to the office, she couldn't remember ever seeing her cousin look so shaky or pale. Nicky jumped down from the chair. His claws clicked on the wood floor and when he reached his owner, he placed his chin on her knee and looked up at her with sympathetic eyes. Lin reached down and patted his head.

While she waited for Viv to return, Lin absentmindedly flipped through a newspaper that someone had left behind on the table. Wondering how long Viv would be with the officer, she kept flicking her eyes towards the aisle. After more than thirty minutes had passed, Lin received a text from her cousin.

Come to my office.

Lin knocked on the office door and a tiny voice told her to come in.

Viv, her face red, was sitting at her desk in the cramped space. "I'm flustered." She let out a long breath. "I wanted to sit here for a few minutes before going back out to the floor."

Lin sat in the office chair next to the desk. "How

did it go?"

"He asked what you'd expect," Viv said. "Why was I at the docks? Why did I run away? Do I know Greg Hammond? How do I know him?"

"You told the officer about Hammond's harassment?"

"I did." Viv rolled her eyes. "And I guess it sounded pretty odd, too, because I got a disbelieving look and some mild berating for not reporting it since running into Hammond all the time bothered me so much."

"Really?" Lin shook her head disappointed at the officer's reaction.

"If I decide to go off-island, then I'm supposed to let the police know." Viv's jaw set and her eyes clouded. "So now I'm a murder suspect."

Lin's hand flew nervously over her hair. "How can they suspect you? Hammond was the one who instigated contact. You didn't want anything to do with him. You always tried to avoid him."

"Try telling that to the police." Viv put her elbows on the table and placed her chin in one hand. She moaned. "What am I going to do?"

Lin's worried eyes flicked about the room and then she looked back at her cousin with resolve. "*We're* going to find the killer. Together."

Viv blinked at Lin and then she nodded. "We know the island. We know lots of people." She looked hopeful.

"You'll hear people talking in the bookstore.

Listen for possible clues." In a half-second, Lin's expression shifted from eager to serious. "I have to tell you something." She proceeded to relay the information about the disappearing man in her photograph and how she spotted him standing near Greg Hammond's boat. "I haven't seen ghosts for twenty years. I was always able to keep them from appearing by thinking of myself surrounded by an impenetrable fog, but it doesn't work anymore. I can't stop them from showing themselves."

Viv's forehead scrunched. "What does it mean? Why can't you stop them anymore? Why is a ghost showing up now? What does this old man have to do with the murder?"

Lin held her hands out palm side up and shrugged. "I don't like it," she whispered. "Why can't I make him go away?"

Viv bit her lower lip. "There are a lot of strange happenings going on."

Lin looked at her watch and jumped from her seat. "Oh. I have a carpenter coming to the house for Nicky's doggy door. I need to go."

The girls made plans to meet for dinner at Viv's house so that they could put together a plan of action about how to figure things out.

Lin rushed from the office, called Nicky to come with her, and the two hurried out of the bookstore and ran up Main Street to their cottage.

CHAPTER 6

Tearing down Vestry Road, Lin could see a man getting into a truck that was parked in front of her house. She and the dog picked up speed and reached the vehicle just as the engine started. Sweat clung to Lin's skin and a small bead of perspiration rolled down the side of her cheek. Leaning towards the truck's open window and gasping, she tried to speak. "I'm ... sorry I'm late," she puffed.

The carpenter opened the door and stepped out.

"I got tied up in town." Lin's legs felt rubbery from the run home, but getting a look at the man standing before her made her even weaker. She cursed herself for being late and arriving drenched in sweat. Staring at the handsome carpenter, she couldn't keep a sigh of regret from slipping from her throat.

The man was tall and fit and his muscles showed clearly under his T-shirt. His dark brown hair was well-cut and he wore it slightly longer showing a bit of wave. Lin was surprised at her reaction to him.

Since her boyfriend broke up with her, she'd had no interest in dating.

"It's okay." He gave her a warm smile. "I left your number back at my house, so I couldn't call to see if you were running late."

"Well, I'm glad I caught you."

"Jeff Whitney." He extended his hand and shook with Lin. She nearly swooned at his touch, but managed to remain upright.

"Carolin Coffin." She didn't know why she introduced herself with her full name. "Everyone calls me, Lin." She wanted to run into the house, shower, change, and fix her hair.

Nicky wagged his little tail. Jeff bent to pat the dog. "So. A doggy door."

Lin nodded as she unlocked the cottage's front door and led the man and dog into the living room. "I thought it could go here." She indicated the door leading to the deck.

The carpenter looked it over and then noticed the door in the kitchen. "Why not place the doggy door in the exit leading from the kitchen? If you'll be living here in the winter when things are wet and messy, it might be better to have all the mud and muck contained in the kitchen rather than in your living room." He looked down at the dog. "What do you think, buddy?" Jeff turned his warm brown eyes to Lin. "Just a suggestion."

Lin considered and then she nodded. "It's a good suggestion. It makes sense." *At least one thing makes sense,* she thought, *because a lot of things that have happened recently don't make any sense at all.*

The trio walked into the kitchen so that Jeff could take some measurements. Nicky supervised the proceedings by watching the man's every move.

"Would you like some coffee or tea or some seltzer?" Lin offered, hoping a drink might cause the good-looking carpenter to stay a few minutes longer.

"Some seltzer would be great." Jeff wrote some numbers on an invoice and did some calculations. He circled the total cost for supplies and labor and turned the paper for Lin to see.

She smiled. "That's very reasonable. I'm relieved that it's in my budget."

Nicky had turned and was focused on something in the living room. He let out a low whine.

"What's up, buddy? You want your door in the living room?" Jeff asked.

Lin crossed to the threshold and followed the dog's gaze across the room. Her eyes nearly fell out of their sockets. She let out a gasp and then masked it by coughing a few times.

The eighteenth-century man was standing in the living room next to a shimmering woman who wore a long dress with a high collar. Her hair was neatly done up in a low bun which sat at the back of her neck. A few wavy tendrils fell softly around her face. She was in a sitting position floating a foot above the floor, a kind look on her face.

If Nicky can see the ghosts.... Lin's head swiveled to Jeff, back to the ghosts, and then turned to Jeff again. He seemed unaware of the uninvited guests. Relieved, she gave him a goofy smile trying to cover her shock at having two ghosts in the living room.

"Everything okay?" Jeff asked.

"Uh, huh." Lin hurried back to the kitchen. "Let me get you that cold drink." She bustled in the refrigerator, her mind going a mile a minute. *Now what? Who are they? Why can't I stop ghosts from appearing?* Her stomach felt cold and tight. She wouldn't look back into the living room. Just as she was pouring the seltzer into a glass, the ghost-woman floated into the kitchen and hovered close to the carpenter looking at him with interest.

Lin's heart sank. *Go away.* She put a slice of lemon on the rim of the glass and passed the drink to Jeff.

The ghost-woman eyed the man from top to bottom and then gave Lin a nod. Lin's eyes were like saucers.

Jeff asked, "So should I schedule the doggy door for the end of the week?"

"What?" Lin pried her eyes away from the floating ghost. "Yes, the end of the week is good." She gave the man a sweet smile.

Jeff drained his seltzer and rinsed the glass in the sink. "I'll see you then. I'll give you a call tomorrow."

Lin's face brightened.

"I'll let you know what time and if the installation will be Thursday or Friday." He shook her hand.

Walking Jeff to the door, Lin thanked him for his time and told him she looked forward to having the door installed. As soon as the cottage door was shut, she whirled to confront the ghosts who were both floating near the threshold to the kitchen. "Who are you?" Lin demanded. She took several steps forward. "Why are you here?"

The man and woman's shimmering atoms began to swirl and fade and then the man was gone, but just before the woman disappeared she gave Lin a little wave.

The room was empty. Nicky wagged his tail still staring at the spots where the ghosts had stood.

Lin stomped her foot and put her hands on her hips. "Arrghh," she roared in frustration.

CHAPTER 7

With Nicky at her heels, Lin opened the gate beneath the trellis of the white picket fence and stepped along the stone walkway to the front door of Viv's Cape Cod style house. The shingles on the cottage, a Nantucket tradition, had weathered to a soft silver-gray. Pink roses spilled over the fence. The front door and the shutters on each side of the windows were a soft shade of robin's-egg blue. Flowers overflowed from the window boxes. Lin stepped to the door and rang the bell.

She heard Viv call for her to come inside.

Nicky trotted in, put his nose against the wood floor, and sniffed around trying to find Queenie. The cat, sitting upright on the back of the sofa, watched the dog rush past oblivious to the feline's presence. The cat lay down and studied the furry animal hurrying to and fro about the room. As she waited for the dog to discover her, Queenie made eye contact with Lin.

Lin glanced at the silly dog rushing about, grinned at the cat, shrugged a shoulder, and shook her head.

Viv greeted her cousin with a warm smile. Standing at the kitchen counter, she rubbed garlic over sliced Italian bread and then drizzled it with olive oil.

Lin placed a platter on the table and gave Viv a hug. "I brought a green salad with pecans, strawberries, and goat's cheese. It smells delicious in here." She inhaled deeply. "Wow, you had time to make lasagna?"

"Cooking always seems to calm me."

"Well, I'm glad it does because then I get a tasty meal." Lin grinned as she removed two wine glasses from the cabinet.

Viv placed the cookie sheet with the bread into the oven. "I left the bookstore early. I was a bundle of nerves and good for nothing, so I came home. Anyway, I had to meet a workman who is going to repair some wall boards near the fireplace."

An uncomfortable sense of cold flashed through Lin's body when Viv mentioned the fireplace. She shook herself. "What's wrong with the wall?"

"The boards are bulging out for some reason. A bit of the wall has to be opened up and new boards put in. It's an old house, things always need to be fixed or replaced."

"That's the beauty of antique homes." Lin smiled as she put the wine glasses on a tray. The girls often complained about all the things that needed attention when living in an older home.

"John can't make it for dinner. He has to meet clients this evening which is just as well because now we can talk freely about things." Viv raised an eyebrow and gave her cousin a pointed look.

"Did you tell him about the police officer's visit to see you today?" Lin poured wine into the glasses.

Viv gave a nod. "I tried to downplay it, but John's worried. I assured him that the killer would be caught soon and everything will be fine." She looked up from her task, her eyes heavy with concern. "I wish I could convince myself."

When the meal was ready, the girls carried their plates and glasses out to the deck and sat down at the wooden table. One side of the deck was attached to an ell that jutted off the back of Viv's house. The ell, original to the house, was a one story structure that once housed a kitchen, but now was used for storage. Two sides of the deck were open to the yard and gardens. The sun had fallen behind the trees at the back of Viv's small property and the air carried a refreshing coolness that caused Lin to put on her sweater.

"Have you come up with any ideas about why ghosts are suddenly appearing out of the blue?" Viv took a sip of her wine.

Lin shook her head. She told her cousin about the latest ghosts to materialize in her house. "I nearly had a stroke when the ghost-woman floated into the kitchen and anchored herself right next to the carpenter. I couldn't focus on anything he was saying." She made a sad face. "He probably thinks I'm a nut."

"More likely, he didn't even notice your distress." Viv rubbed her forehead. "Why don't you talk to these ghosts? Ask them what's going on around here. Can't they be helpful and not just stand around staring at you?"

Lin sighed. "It doesn't work that way. They say what they want, when they want."

"Have you ever tried asking them a question?"

Lin narrowed her eyes. She couldn't remember ever asking a spirit a question when she was little. It had been so long ago when spirits revealed themselves to her on a regular basis, but no, she was pretty sure she had never asked any of them a question. "Not when I was little. I don't think I ever did. Today I asked the ghosts some questions, but I was angry and they disappeared."

"Maybe you should try asking things in a tactful way. Be polite, respectful." Viv lifted a forkful of lasagna to her mouth.

Lin had a feeling that wouldn't work.

Viv looked out at the back of her garden and let out a long sigh. "Why on earth would Greg Hammond be so determined to own this place? It's cute and well-tended, but so are all the other houses around here. The house is old, but again, so are the other places in the neighborhood. The house and property are small. There isn't room to expand. Why was his interest so intense?"

Lin swallowed a bite of garlic bread and glanced about the backyard. "Have you seen any ghosts around here?"

Viv's eyes bugged out. "Me?" Her eyes flicked nervously around the lawn area and her shoulders hunched together. "*I* can't see ghosts." Her voice held a slight tone of panic. "*You* see ghosts." Hesitating for a second, she asked, "Can you see any?"

"No, but I wonder..."

Viv leaned forward. "What? What do you wonder?"

"I feel like these things have to be related. Greg Hammond was so desperate to get his hands on your house, me seeing ghosts again, the murder. It can't be coincidence."

"Then what is it?" Viv gave Lin a worried look.

"It seems that it all centers on this house. I know that it's been in the family for generations, but what is it about this particular house? We don't know much about it really. Do you know more about its history than I do?"

Viv's shoulders relaxed and her tension seemed to ease. "It was built in the early 1700's and was owned by several members of Grandma's family before she inherited it. When she got sick, my mom bought it from Grandma and she and dad moved in to take care of her. Your mom and dad were living on the mainland at the time. My mom had a great desire to own the house of her ancestors so she convinced dad they should buy it. Then my parents left it to me. That's about all I know."

"So," Lin tapped her chin, thinking. "Is it something from the past that Hammond was after? Or is it something more recent? Did Grandma or your parents leave something valuable in the house?"

Viv's eyes went wide. "Like what?"

"Hidden money, jewelry?"

"No." Viv rolled her eyes. "You know there isn't anything valuable in here."

"In the attic?" Lin tilted her head.

Viv scowled. "The attic? It's not very big. You can't even stand up in there. You have to hunch over. I don't know what's up there. Probably nothing."

"Maybe we should go look."

Viv wrinkled her nose and groaned. "I hate attics." She shook her head. "Not tonight. I'm too wound up from the day." She gave her cousin a look. "We'll do it another time."

Darkness had fallen around them. A sudden cool wind blew across the yard. The candle on the table flickered, sputtered, and burned out. Viv took a quick look to the sky, alarmed. She reached for her plate and glass, ready to hurry back inside the house.

"Wait," Lin whispered. She felt something on the air and looked to the fence that ran along the property line between Viv's garden and the yard of the old mansion on the other side of the fence. It almost seemed like words were floating on the breeze, but Lin couldn't make them out.

Viv peered over her shoulders into the dark yard. She kept her voice low. "I want to go in." She leaned forward. "Lin. Now."

"Hold on." Lin thought that she could sense something trying to materialize. She sighed when the feeling passed. "It's only the wind. Don't be so jumpy."

Viv kept flicking her eyes around the dark yard.

"Do you think this whole mess could have something to do with our ancestors?" Lin fiddled with her glass. The cousins' ancestors had been among the early founders of the island and some had been prominent figures in Nantucket's whaling industry.

"How do you mean?" Viv narrowed her eyes.

"That spirit who shows up in eighteenth-century clothes makes me think that all this stuff that's been going on must have some link to our past."

"This whole thing is giving me a headache." Viv leaned back against her chair. "We need to start investigating Hammond's murder. Listen to conversations. Ask people questions. Ghosts don't seem to be any help. We need to talk to living people to get some answers."

Lin shrugged. She wasn't convinced that ghosts couldn't help, but she didn't say anything about that. "My first landscaping jobs start tomorrow. I'll bring up the murder and see what people have to say. Any little thing can lead to important information. We'll keep our ears open." Lin gave her cousin a smile. "We'll get to the bottom of it. We're a good team."

Even though worry was etched across her forehead, Viv nodded. "Let's go clean up."

Lin gathered her dishes and as she followed her cousin into the house, she looked back over the dark garden. *I know you're there. What do you want?*

CHAPTER 8

Lin pulled her truck into the driveway of an antique Cape-style house, her last stop of the day. The sun beat down on her as she grabbed her work bag out of the back of the truck and then let Nicky out of the passenger side. The little brown dog wagged his tail and followed Lin to the door, where she rang the bell. She preferred to alert the homeowners before she headed into the gardens to work so as not to alarm them when they spied someone in their yards.

No one answered the bell, so Lin walked down the steps and followed the brick walkway around to the back of the property. A large bluestone patio stood behind the house and pots of different sizes filled with flowers had been placed around the area. A border of pink and white impatiens, red geraniums, and pink and white cleome ran along the edge of the lawn.

Lin started at one end of the patio pots picking out dead blooms and tossing them into a container she'd brought along. While she unrolled a garden hose to water the pots, Nicky trotted around the patio and the small lawn sniffing out the new smells. When the dog let out a woof of surprise, Lin dropped the hose and whirled around to see an older man emerge from the trees on the far side of the lawn.

The gray-haired, skinny, wiry man carried a pair of hedge clippers and he waved as he approached the patio. "Hello. You must be the new gardener." He gave a warm smile and extended his hand. "Anton Wilson."

Nicky hid behind Lin which puzzled the young woman. Goosebumps formed along her arms. She couldn't remember ever seeing the dog act so cautiously and his behavior unnerved her.

She shook hands with the man. "Lin Coffin."

"Coffin? I don't remember hearing your last name. You're a Coffin, are you?"

Lin nodded. "My last name isn't on the garden company website or invoices." She eyed the clippers. "Is there some trimming you'd like me to take care of?"

"Oh my, no. I like to putter. I gave the hedges a little trim." He waved to the back of the property. "I just need someone to take care of the watering and weeding. I'm always working and I'm often away so that's why I contracted with you for the flowers."

"Well, if you ever need something extra done, I'd be glad to help out."

"So tell me, which line of the Coffins are you related to?" Wilson looked eagerly at Lin.

"My family is descended from Sebastian Coffin."

Wilson gave a little gasp. "How wonderful. A most intriguing fellow. Not the most famous of the Coffins, but I believe his is the most interesting line of the family." He gave Lin a wink.

"I don't know our history, really. I just know that Sebastian didn't follow the rest of his family into the whaling business back in the day."

"Yes, you're right." Wilson's bushy gray eyebrows rose up his forehead. "But the whaling is the least intriguing part of the family."

"How do you know so much about the Coffins?" Lin cocked her head.

Wilson straightened up. "I'm a historian, my dear. I've written extensively about your family." He looked over at the door to the house. "Do you have time for a cold drink?" He gestured to the patio table. "I can tell you a bit about your family tree."

Lin hesitated, but she was feeling worn out from the long day of outside work. She wasn't used to working in the heat, bending and squatting to weed, and pushing a lawn mower up and down yards. Her legs felt like jelly. A cold drink sounded very good and she wondered if this man who knew so much about the island might have heard some information about the murder of Greg Hammond. "A cold drink would be great."

"Sit, please." Wilson smiled and pulled out one of the lawn chairs. "I'll be back in a flash."

Easing into the chair, Lin was keenly aware of her sore muscles and she knew that the achy feeling would be even worse when she got up the next morning. Her mouth turned up in a tiny grin as she pictured herself limping around the gardens of the next day's customers.

She looked down at her brown dog sitting under the table. "What's wrong with you, Nick? Why don't you come out from under there?" The dog didn't budge.

Just then, Mr. Wilson came out of the house carrying a small tray with two glasses clinking with ice, a jug of iced tea, and a silver bowl filled with sugar cubes. He bustled to the table and set down the tray. "Here we are. I hope you like iced tea." Wilson filled the glasses and handed one to Lin.

She was so hot and sweaty, Lin wanted to pour the cold liquid right over her head, but she controlled herself. She took a sip from the glass. "Wonderful."

"So tell me." Wilson leaned forward eagerly. "Have you lived here on the island your whole life?'

Lin explained that she was born on Nantucket, but that she'd grown up in Cambridge and spent time back on the island with her grandfather during summers and some weekends.

"What was your grandfather's name?"

"Elliot Coffin."

Wilson tapped his fingers on the surface of the wood table. "Ah. I knew him slightly from town events.

"And your father?"

"His name was Elliot, as well."

"You know, I have some research in the house. Some day you must stay after tending the gardens and I'll show you your family tree. I think you'll find it most interesting." He tilted his head. "Do you have siblings?"

Lin shook her head. "My parents passed away when I was only a year old."

"I'm sorry," Wilson murmured. "So then you are Elliot's firstborn."

Lin raised an eyebrow at the comment wondering why the older man mentioned that she was her father's first and only child. She waited for him to elaborate.

Wilson studied the young woman's face. "Your grandfather raised you?"

"He did."

"Interesting. And what about your mother?"

"Her name was Merry Witchard."

Wilson almost leapt from his seat with excitement. "Then you are both a Witchard and a Coffin. My, my. In my opinion, the Witchard family is the most fascinating of all the early founders." His voice was breathless. "Yes, fascinating." Wilson's gray-blue eyes ran over the curves and edges of Lin's face. His gaze didn't hold any warmth or desire, his visual scrutiny was more like a clinical inspection of a specimen and it made Lin want to move away from him.

The young woman pushed her chair back. "I'd better get going. I have another stop to make," she lied. "Thank you for the iced tea." She stood.

Wilson got up. "When you return at the end of the week, please stay and we can go over your family trees." He gave Lin a pointed look. "I do think you'll enjoy hearing about your family histories."

"That sounds good. It was nice to meet you." Lin picked up her bag of tools and walked briskly to the front of the house. "Come on, Nick."

The little dog scooted out from under the patio table and rocketed past his owner down the front walkway to their truck.

CHAPTER 9

Lin was covered in sweat and she had grass and soil pressed into the knees of her jeans as she hurried into Viv's bookstore with Nicky at her heels. She wanted to talk to her cousin about Anton Wilson. Striding to the back of the store expecting to see Viv at the beverage counter, Lin nearly collided with someone stepping into the aisle from behind one of the bookshelves.

"I'm sorry." Lin stopped her forward momentum just in time to keep from plowing into the person. "I wasn't paying attention."

"You're in quite a hurry, Carolin." It was the white-haired woman who had known Lin's grandfather. Lin had met her the other morning at the bookstore just before they'd heard that someone had been killed down at the docks.

Lin couldn't recall the woman's name and silently reprimanded herself for not paying closer attention when she'd introduced herself. "Oh, hi. I'm looking for Viv."

"I saw her leave a little while ago." The woman

scrutinized Lin's face. "Is everything okay? You seem a little ... frazzled."

Lin blinked. She could see concern in the woman's blue eyes, but there was something else showing that Lin couldn't put her finger on. She shook herself wondering if Greg Hammond's obsession with Viv's house and his murder was making her suspicious and paranoid of the people around her. "I've been working outside in the hot sun all day. I'm just worn out. I could really use a shower."

"I thought I saw your truck parked in front of Anton Wilson's house. Do you garden for him?"

"Today was my first day. There are a number of prior clients that remained with the business after I took it over. Mr. Wilson's house was my last stop." Lin wiped her dirty palm on her jeans.

The woman took a step closer. "Have you met Anton?"

"I met him today. He was in the backyard when I got there."

"What did you think of him?"

Lin thought that was a strange question. "He was very pleasant."

The woman cocked her head. "Did he have questions for you?"

Lin shifted from foot to foot, wondering what this interrogation was about and why the woman had such keen interest in her interaction with Wilson. She forced a chuckle. "Does Mr. Wilson have a reputation for questioning people he has just met?"

"Anton can be an odd duck." The woman adjusted the collar of her crisp white shirt.

"Can he?" Lin shrugged a shoulder. "Well. I guess I'll head home now since Viv isn't here."

The woman nodded. "Nice to see you." As she stepped away to another shelf of books, she spoke over her shoulder. "Keep your wits about you, Carolin."

A little shiver ran down Lin's back as she hurried out of the bookstore. When she was outside on the sidewalk and heading up Main Street, she took out her phone and texted her cousin. A minute later, Lin received a reply from Viv saying she was with John, but was heading home now and that Lin could meet her at the house. Lin and Nicky turned at the next corner to walk the four blocks to Viv's neighborhood and they reached the house just as Viv pulled up on her bike.

"What happened to you?" Viv got off the bicycle. "Did you fall into a pile of dirt?"

"Very funny." Lin scowled.

Nicky danced around Viv's legs begging for a scratch on the head and she bent to oblige. She looked up at her cousin. "How was the first day as a professional gardener?"

Lin groaned. "I'm sure I won't be able to move tomorrow. I didn't think I was in such bad shape."

Viv chuckled. "You're in great shape. You just

haven't used these particular muscles very much. In a week you'll be fine."

"Or I'll be dead in a week." Lin limped along following Viv around the side of the house to the backyard.

Viv leaned her bike against the tool shed. "You want to use my shower?" She eyed her cousin. "You're filthy."

Lin shook her head. "I'm going home in a bit. Can we sit out here? I want to talk for a minute."

The girls sat at the patio table while Nicky ran about the yard with his nose to the ground.

"Have you found out something about Greg Hammond's murder?" Viv's eyes widened with excitement.

"No. I haven't made any progress on that front."

Viv looked deflated.

"Who is the pretty older woman who was in your store the other day? White hair, layered around the face, blue eyes. She was there the day we heard about Hammond's murder. She was with three other older people."

"That's Libby Hartnett. They all come in every morning, have coffee, a muffin. They chat, gossip. That's how they start their day."

"Is she ... odd?"

Viv's face scrunched in confusion. "Why do say that?"

"They knew me, you know. They said they knew Grandpa. Did Grandpa usually meet with them at the bookstore?"

"Yeah." Viv nodded. "Most mornings. They were all friends." She narrowed her eyes. "Why are you asking?"

Lin blew out a breath and told Viv about Anton Wilson and his apparent keen interest in sharing family history details with her and then about running into Libby Hartnett at the bookstore and what she'd said. "Why would Libby be so interested in what Anton talked to me about?"

"I don't know." Viv looked off across the yard, thinking.

"And why would she tell me to keep my wits about me?"

Viv made eye contact with her cousin. "That's very odd. What's going on?"

"What do you know about Anton Wilson and Libby Hartnett?"

"Not a whole lot." Viv put her chin in her hand and leaned her elbow on top of the table. "Wilson is a former professor, retired now. I can't remember where he taught. He's written a million books about Nantucket. He's something of an expert on the island and the inhabitants. Wilson is on the Historical Commission. He gives talks and lectures all over the mainland."

"So he's reputable? Not a nut?"

"Quirky, I'd say. Intense, but I've never heard anyone complain that he's nuts. I think he would just love to have been descended from one of the founding families of the island."

"And Libby? What do you know about her?"

"Less than I know about Wilson. She's lived here all of her life. She's quiet, polite. Spends time raising money for island charities, to help the schools, the hospital, the arts. I think her family owned a farm here, but I'm not sure about that. She loves to read, she's always buying books. She's a good customer."

"Why would she tell me to keep my wits about me?" Lin's stomach felt cold and empty. "Is she warning me about something?"

Nicky joined the girls on the deck and he rubbed his head against Lin's leg.

"I have no idea what she meant." Viv gave a weary sigh. "But it wouldn't hurt for either one of us to keep our heads up and be careful."

A thought popped into Lin's head and her eyes clouded. "Libby said she saw my truck parked at Anton Wilson's house. How does she know my truck?"

Viv's face looked pinched, but after a few seconds her features relaxed. "Libby was friends with your granddad. She knew his truck. She must assume you inherited it."

Lin relaxed. "That's a relief. I wondered if she was stalking me." She reached down to pat Nicky's head. "Have you been following the news stories about Hammond? It seems like the guy was sort of a loner. No wife, no kids. Had his business, his boat, but that seemed to be all."

"There don't seem to be any leads in the killing." Viv pushed her hair behind her ears. "According to the news reports, anyway." She blinked a few times. "It worries me. Are they going to try to pin Hammond's murder on me?"

Lin put her hand on her cousin's arm. "You're innocent. They can't arrest you for this. There's no evidence."

Tears gathered in Viv's eyes. "I hate this whole mess. What are the connections? Are any of these things connected? Hammond's desire to buy my house, his murder, the ghosts." She looked at her cousin. "Have you seen any more ghosts?"

"Only the times I've told you about." Lin was glad that she hadn't had more visits from spirits. She changed the subject. "Did you get the wall fixed near the fireplace yet?"

Viv gave a long sigh. "It turns out there are boards and plaster over a hollow section in the wall. The workman thinks there's an old cupboard there that somebody closed up long ago. He called it a parson's cupboard, or something like that."

A cold breeze washed over Lin's skin and she gave herself a little shake.

"He's coming back to work on it. Of course, it's more involved than what was originally thought, which means more money than I originally thought."

Lin nodded sympathetically and joked. "Ah, the

beauty of owning an antique home."

They both chuckled.

The two girls sat in silence for several minutes, and then Lin said, "I guess I'll head home and get cleaned up. I think we need to go down to the docks and ask around about Greg Hammond. See what we can find out. Tomorrow morning before I start work, I'm going to drive out to Hammond's landscape business and see if there's anyone there I can talk to."

"Be careful. Text me and let me know what's going on."

The girls walked to the front of Viv's house. Lin gave her cousin a hug and then she and the dog walked up the sidewalk for home.

CHAPTER 10

The early morning sun peeking over the tall trees hit Lin right in the eyes as she drove toward Greg Hammond's landscape business. She pulled her sunglasses off the console and slipped them on. As she predicted, her muscles were killing her from yesterday's gardening. She hoped they'd loosen up as she worked once she headed to her first client. If her muscles stayed tight and sore, she was in for a very long day.

Nicky was in the passenger seat. He had his paws resting on the armrest so he could move his nose up closer to the crack in the window. Lin was afraid the dog would lose his balance and fall out if the window was down all the way, so she only opened it a couple of inches.

A sign on the left side of the road indicated Hammond Landscaping, so Lin turned her truck into the gravel lot and parked next to a small cottage that was used as the office. Before getting out, she looked around the property. Behind the office, there were several trucks parked beside four large greenhouses and a section of the space contained potted trees and plants lined up in rows.

No one was in sight so Lin and Nicky got out of the truck and walked to the office. Expecting the door to be locked, she was surprised when she turned the knob and the door opened. It was a small space with a couple of orange plastic chairs pushed against the wall near the entrance and a waist-high counter stood at the other side of the room.

"Hello?" Lin looked around the space. There was a door to a back office with a sign on it that said, "Bookkeeping – Employees Only."

No one answered.

An old wooden desk was placed against the wall behind the counter. A calendar hung from a loose screw on the wall. Next to a rusty metal lamp on the desk stood a gold metal nameplate with the words *Greg Hammond, Proprietor* engraved onto it and attached to a wooden holder. Papers and folders were strewn over the desk's surface with a stray pen and pencil and a few paper clips scattered here and there.

The door behind Lin opened with a thud causing her to jump.

"You need something?" A tall skinny man with a dark tan and a scruffy beard stood just inside the open door. His jeans and T-shirt had smudges of soil on them. "The place is closed today."

"Oh." Lin blinked. "I didn't see a sign."

"That's 'cuz there isn't one. You a customer?"

"I wanted to buy some plants."

"You can't. The place is closed." The guy narrowed his eyes at Lin and his creepy gaze gave her a shiver.

Nicky stepped around and stood in front of his owner to block the man from getting closer.

"Is Mr. Hammond around?" Lin pretended she didn't know anything about the events of the past few days.

"He's dead."

"Oh." Lin feigned surprise. "I'm sorry to hear that."

"Yeah, I'm sure Greg is, too." The guy chuckled. His open mouth showed missing teeth and the few he did have were broken, yellow, and crooked.

Sweat dribbled down Lin's back. She wanted to recoil from the awful man, but she kept her face neutral. "Are you the manager?"

"I'm the worker."

Lin decided that this guy would be the first to go if she ran this landscaping business. "Is the business being sold?"

"Yeah."

"Who's handling the sale?"

"How do I know?" The man's voice was gruff. "The lawyer, I suppose. You need to go. I got work to do."

Lin started for the exit giving the rude employee wide berth. "Come on, Nick." When she glanced down expecting the dog to be at her feet, Nicky wasn't there. She heard rustling behind the counter and hurried over to look. The dog was snuffling under the desk and ignored Lin when she called a second time.

Walking around the counter, she bent to fish the dog out from under the wooden workspace. Just as she lifted Nicky, her gaze spotted a book on the floor that must have slipped from the desktop. When she read the title and author, she narrowed her eyes.

Ghost Mysteries of Nantucket by Anton Wilson.

A little shiver of unease washed over the young woman as she was about to carry her dog out of the office. In her hurry, she almost bumped into a husky man who was entering the building. The guy looked familiar to Lin. He had a patch sewn onto his blue work shirt with the words *Bill Ward, Manager - Hammond Landscaping* embroidered on the oval.

"You need some help?" The man looked at Lin with heavy-lidded, dark brown eyes. His light brown hair was tinged with streaks of gray and his face was lined from years of outside work. The manager eyed the guy standing just behind Lin. "You got some work to do, Leonard?"

Leonard, the creep, slunk away to the back room of the office.

The manager kept his voice low. "Leonard doesn't have much in the way of social graces. Can

I answer any questions for you?"

Lin gestured to the retreating Leonard. "He said the business is closed."

"Just for today. We're doing inventory. The business is in the process of being sold, hopefully to me. Right now, we're reorganizing and finishing up the contracts we already have. In a couple of weeks, I'll be able to start taking new business."

"I'm interested in having some stonework done in my yard. A walkway and some stonewalls." Lin made this up and she had no intention of hiring Hammond Landscaping. "I've heard good things about your work. I wondered if I might get a few customer names so I could speak with them about the work that was done for them."

"Sure." The manager led Lin back inside the office. He moved to the desk and the toe of his boot hit Anton Wilson's book that was resting on the floor. He bent and picked up it, placing the book facedown on the desk. He pulled open a file cabinet that stood to the left of the desk and he rummaged through some files. When the manager found what he was looking for, he wrote three names, addresses, and phone numbers on a piece of paper which he handed to Lin. "These folks don't mind being contacted for testimonials."

"Okay, thanks." As Lin was folding the paper to put in her jeans pocket, she recalled that she'd seen Bill down at the docks on the morning of the murder. "Sorry about Mr. Hammond."

Bill stiffened. "Yeah. Well, stuff happens."

Lin got the impression that the manager-soon-to-be-owner wasn't too broken up over the death of his employer. A shiver of disgust ran through her body. "I thought you looked familiar. You were down by Greg's boat the morning of the murder, weren't you?"

Bill looked surprised. "The cops called here after they found the body. I answered. Greg didn't have family. The police asked me to come down."

A whoosh of cold air drifted over Lin. Her heart sank. She knew what it meant and she steeled herself for what she would see. Standing right behind the manager in the far corner of the room was the eighteenth-century ghost. Lin forced her face to stay neutral.

An auburn-haired, middle-aged woman carrying a briefcase opened the door to the building and stepped into the office. She acknowledged Bill and gave Lin a hasty nod.

"This is Joan," Bill said. "She's the bookkeeper."

Joan turned to Bill. "I have that paperwork you wanted to go over." She went through the door to the back office.

"Drop by or give us a call after you talk to those people on the list I gave you." Bill gestured to the paper Lin still held in her hand. "We'd be glad to do the stonework for you. We'll come out and give you an estimate. Let us know as soon as you can and we'll get your job on the work-list."

Lin nodded and thanked the man. Before she and Nicky left the building, Lin took a quick look to the corner. The ghost was gone. Once outside, she thought about the coincidence of finding Anton Wilson's book on ghosts under Greg Hammond's desk.

Walking to her truck, she decided that it might be a good idea to get a copy of that book.

***

Lin, Viv, and Nicky strolled towards the docks. The sun was sinking lower in the sky and the air was much cooler than it had been during the afternoon. Viv had a canvas bag looped over her shoulder. "I brought you the book. I haven't read it. I wonder what mysteries Anton Wilson thinks can be found on the island."

"It's an odd coincidence that Hammond had Wilson's book in his office. I can't wait to look through it."

The girls headed to the section of the docks where Viv's boyfriend John kept his boat. Nicky trotted along after them.

"So John said the guy who used to berth his boat next to Greg Hammond's boat has moved to the slip next to John. John called me this morning before he took the ferry back to the mainland. He's going to Boston to visit his brother for a week. He was surprised to see a different boat beside his when he woke up this morning."

"What's this guy's name?"

"Nate Johnson. He told the Harbor Master that if he couldn't move his boat, then he'd leave the island. John thinks he was freaked out by Hammond's murder and he didn't want to be anywhere near where it happened."

"Some people are superstitious." Lin kept looking over her shoulder. The last time she was at the docks she saw the ghost and she was hoping that he wouldn't make a reappearance.

Viv led the way along the docks. "John said we should use his boat and maybe we'll get a chance to talk to Nate Johnson about the murder. We'll have to be subtle though. We don't want to scare him off."

"Do you know anything about Johnson?"

"I've met him a few times, but I really don't know anything about him."

When the girls reached John's boat they climbed aboard with Lin carrying the dog. Viv went down into the hold and put some things in the refrigerator. She returned with a bottle of wine and some cheese and crackers. She set them down on the table. "Maybe we can entice the new neighbor over for a drink."

The girls settled on the seats and Nicky jumped up to sit next to Lin.

"You think he'll show?"

"Don't turn around but I think he's coming." Viv

smiled and waved to someone on the dock. When the person came closer, she stood, and gave the man a welcome. "Have time to join us for a drink? Wine or beer?" Viv's warm and cheerful personality always drew people in. "John's away for a few days."

Nate Johnson came aboard. He was about six feet tall with sandy blonde hair. Lin estimated that he was probably in his late-thirties. Viv handed him a beer and he sat down.

"So you moved slips?" Viv didn't waste any time bringing up the subject.

"Yeah." Nate didn't elaborate.

"I can't remember," Viv said. "Which dock were you on before this one?"

Nate told them.

"Too noisy over there? Trouble with neighbors?" Viv sipped from her glass.

"That wasn't the problem," Nate said. "I'd been over there for a couple of years. I thought a change was in order."

Lin sighed inwardly afraid that this conversation was going to lead nowhere. "Wasn't that the dock where Greg Hammond had his boat?"

Nate blanched. He took a swig from his bottle of beer. "Yeah." He took another long swallow.

"What did you think of Hammond?" Viv asked as nonchalantly as possible.

"He was okay. Pretty much kept to himself. We'd shoot the breeze now and then."

Lin patted Nicky. "Was he the type who courted trouble? Or do you think the attack was random?"

Nate seemed to wince, and then he shook his head. "I don't think it was random. I think Greg got mixed up in some kind of mess."

"Drugs?" Lin asked even though she doubted that was at the root of the killing.

"Nah. Greg wasn't into stuff like that."

"What do you think it was about then?" Viv leaned slightly forward trying to encourage speculation. She offered the man another beer thinking that more drink might loosen his tongue.

"Greg was into get-rich-quick schemes. He was always reading about things he could do to make extra money."

"Why?" Lin looked puzzled. "He had a big landscaping business. Didn't that keep him busy? It must have done well."

Nate scratched the back of his neck. He shifted in his seat. "Greg was pressed for money. He ... well, he had a bit of a gambling problem. Money slipped through his fingers pretty easy."

Lin's eyes widened. "You think Hammond was killed over a gambling debt?"

Nate was quiet for a few moments. "If I had to guess? It's possible. He was messing with some dangerous characters. That's one of the reasons I wanted to move my boat over here." Nate shook his head. "But, who knows? He could've been killed over something else."

"Were you around that morning?" Perspiration formed on Viv's forehead. Just thinking about being down on the dock and hearing the arguing voices on the morning of the murder made her break out in a sweat.

Nate nodded. "I was down below. I was making breakfast."

"Did you hear anything? See anything?" Lin pressed.

Viv hoped that Nate hadn't seen her walking past on the docks that day.

"I heard some shouting. I couldn't hear what they were saying. I wasn't sure if it was somebody fooling around, or maybe a television was on, something like that." Nate looked down at his hands. "I was the one who found the body. I should've gone over there right away when I heard the noise, but I didn't. After I ate my breakfast, I felt uneasy about the yelling I heard, so I went over to Greg's boat, called for him. He didn't answer. I could smell something burning inside so I went in. There was a frying pan on the stove. Greg was facedown on the floor." He made eye contact with the girls. "That's the real reason I moved slips."

"I'm so sorry," Viv said.

Everyone was silent for a minute.

"Did you see anyone around that morning?" Lin asked quietly.

Viv's throat tightened waiting for the man's answer hoping he hadn't seen her pass by.

"No one I'd consider a murderer."

"You *did* see someone though?" Lin's face was serious.

"Yeah. Before I went below to make my breakfast, I saw that charity lady. That older woman. Mrs. Hartnett's her name. She was walking on the dock. I nodded to her before I went down to make breakfast."

Libby Hartnett? "Does she have a boat down here?" Lin's eyebrows knitted together.

Nate shook his head. "I figured she must be down to pester some big wig into making a donation to something or other. I thought it might be something for the Whaling Museum since she had that historical guy with her."

"What historical guy?" Viv eyed the man.

"That writer guy, you know, he's kind of weasely looking. He wrote all those books about Nantucket."

Lin and Viv exchanged a look.

"You're sure they were together?" Lin's heart was beating double-time.

"Well, they were on the dock at the same time. Can't say if they were together or not. Seemed like it, though." Nate drained his beer bottle. "I better get going." He stood up, thanked the girls for the refreshments, and returned to his boat.

"What's that about?" Lin whispered to her cousin. "Anton Wilson and Libby Hartnett on the dock just before Greg Hammond was murdered?"

Her breathing was quick and shallow. For a second, Lin felt cold and she thought she saw something fleeting pass by the stern of John's boat.

Viv's eyes were wide. "There must be an explanation. They must have been down here for some legitimate reason. They couldn't have killed Hammond." She looked over at the other boats lined up along the dock, her face muscles tense. She turned to Lin and said softly, "Could they?"

CHAPTER 11

Lin had been up late doing programming work for the Boston start-up company that she was working for remotely. She tumbled into bed after 1am and when the alarm went off at 5:30 in the morning she wanted to pummel the screeching little box with her pillow.

After a long day of outside work, Lin couldn't wait to get home and shower and then curl up with Anton Wilson's ghost book that Viv had given her the night before. The sun was low in the sky when Lin yawned and turned the truck onto Vestry Road. Her stomach was growling, her head was aching, and her muscles were still screaming from four days of gardening work in the high heat. A light sheen of perspiration covered her skin and smudges of soil and plant matter stuck to her jean shorts from hours of weeding, watering, and mowing.

Approaching her house, she saw a truck parked in front. *Oh, no. The carpenter is still here.* She wondered if there would ever be a day when she talked to the handsome man without looking like she'd been hit by a train. She let out a long sigh as she and Nicky emerged from their vehicle.

When she opened the front door, the little dog tore across the living room and into the kitchen where the man was finishing up the work on the doggy door. The carpenter laughed as the dog danced around and gave the man a swish across his chiseled cheek with a long pink tongue.

"Hey, Nick." Jeff sat back on the floor. "Your door is almost finished." The carpenter pushed the little door to show the dog how to use it. Nicky sniffed, pushed through it to go out onto the deck, and ran into the yard.

"Well, I guess that's a success." Lin chuckled. "I see you found the key to the back door under the rock." She couldn't help but admire the physique of the man sitting on her kitchen floor. His warm smile and deep brown eyes made her heart swell.

Jeff stood up. "In the future, you might want to find a better hiding place for the key. It's kind of in an obvious spot." He gave Lin a smile. "I got here later than I thought. Another job ran over time. That's why I'm still here."

"The doggy door looks great." Lin couldn't stifle a yawn. "Sorry."

"Looks like someone has had a long day." Jeff gathered his tools from the floor and put them in his metal case.

Unable to hide her fatigue and knowing that a guy like Jeff would never be attracted to a dirty, sweat-soaked mess like her, she gave up all thoughts of flirting and sank onto the stool where she leaned forward and put her chin in her hand.

"You okay?" Jeff looked at Lin with concern.

"I can barely move. I was an idiot to think I could handle this gardening job." Lin's eyelids drooped.

Jeff let out a soft chuckle. "You'll get used to it. Don't give up. You look like you're in good shape. Before you know it, you'll be coming home feeling like you could keep working for a few more hours."

Lin narrowed her eyes skeptically.

"Okay. I'll modify that statement. You'll come home in the evening and you won't be dragging. And your muscles won't be burning either."

Lin sucked in a deep breath and let it out. "Really?"

"Really." Jeff snapped the lid shut on the tool case. He eyed Lin. "If you can stay awake long enough, how about you go take a shower and I'll make a run to the farm store and bring back some takeout for us? We've both had a long day and my guess is that we're both starving and neither one of us wants to cook dinner."

The corners of Lin's mouth turned up. "Really?"

"Really." Jeff chuckled. "I'll be back in thirty minutes."

Lin smiled. "It's a deal."

Just then Nicky ran into the kitchen through the doggy door, whooshed in a circle around the room, and darted back outside through his little door leaving Lin and Jeff roaring with laughter at the nutty dog's antics.

"I think he likes it." Lin's eyes sparkled.

***

Her hair still damp from the shower, Lin finished setting the deck table with plates, glasses, and silverware just as Jeff came around the corner of the house carrying a large paper bag full of takeout food.

"It smells delicious." Lin's stomach growled.

They sat at the table eating their food and drinking craft beer with a candle flickering softly on the table in the waning light of the day as they chatted and got to know one another. Jeff had been an Air Force pilot for eight years when he left the service to return to his hometown on Nantucket. He'd considered applying to fly for a commercial airline, but decided he would prefer the quieter lifestyle and natural beauty that his home island provided so he came back and started his business.

Lin shared things about her growing up years, her schooling, first jobs, and her desire to make a permanent home on Nantucket. Throughout their conversation, the small dog asserted his independence by using his doggy door to enter and exit the house at will.

"You heard about the murder down at the

docks?" Jeff lifted his beer glass.

Lin's shoulders tensed up. "I did. Awful."

"Murders are pretty rare around here. I've been wondering what it was all about."

"Did you know Hammond?"

Jeff leaned back in his chair. "Only a little. The business people on the island can be a tight-knit group. Greg never struck me as much of a businessman. He seemed to rely too heavily on his employees."

"Did he ignore his company?"

"I can't say that for certain, but he never seemed too involved with the day-to-day tasks. He had the manager, Bill, running most of it. Bill's wife, Joan, is the bookkeeper and Leonard runs the nursery section."

"Leonard? He's capable of running part of the business?"

"Not sure about that." Jeff shrugged. "Hammond was always off on some new scheme to make money. The guy was fascinated with treasure hunting. He loved diving sunken ships. I think he was pretty sure he was going to hit the jackpot one day. About a year ago, he asked a few of us to join him on a dive in the Caribbean. I refused to go. I thought he was too much of a daredevil, taking stupid risks, putting himself in danger. I had enough of danger serving in the military. That was something I didn't need any more of in my life."

"Someone told me that Hammond had some

trouble with gambling."

"I heard that, too," Jeff said. "I'm not surprised. I think the guy struggled with good judgment. I shouldn't speak ill of the dead, but Greg seemed like someone who could make a mountain of trouble for himself."

Lin hesitated, then decided to tell Jeff about Viv's experience with Hammond. "He was obsessive over her house. He frightened Viv."

Jeff narrowed his eyes, clearly annoyed at Hammond's behavior. "What in the world? Those seem like the actions of a desperate man."

"But what could he have been so desperate over?" Lin questioned.

"What is it about your cousin's house that could have attracted Greg?" Jeff pondered.

"We've been racking our brains trying to figure that out." Lin sighed. "I doubt there's any treasure hidden in some nook or cranny of Viv's antique Cape."

"It's a historical home, but Greg only cared about historical things if he saw a dollar sign hanging from them." Jeff finished his beer.

"You know, I was at Hammond's business the other day." Lin's face was serious. "I went there to see if I could find out anything about Greg and why he was so obsessed with Viv's house." Thinking about the visit she paid to the landscaping company and the two men she'd talked with made Lin shake her head. "I thought Leonard and Bill were kind of odd. Bill didn't seem to care in the least that his employer had been murdered and Leonard seemed to take delight in making me uncomfortable." Lin's lips turned down in distaste. "Anyway, Nicky scooted under a desk in their office and I had to fish him out. When I was trying to grab him, I saw a book on the floor under Hammond's desk. It was about ghost mysteries on Nantucket. You think Greg could have been interested in things like that?"

"I've no idea. If he could make money from something ghost-related then he'd probably be interested." Jeff shrugged. "Did you look through the book?"

"No, I didn't want to linger in that office. Last night, Viv gave me a copy from her bookstore though. I just haven't had time to look at it."

"Is it here?" Jeff's eyes were bright with interest. "Shall we have a look?"

"I left it in the living room." Lin and Jeff got up from the table and went into the house. Lin thought she'd left the book on the side table next to the easy chair, but the tabletop was empty. She bent to see if it had fallen to the floor, maybe knocked there by the dog's exuberant running. "It isn't here." Lin stood up, her hands on her hips, and glanced about the room. "Where could it be?"

"You sure you brought it in? Could it be in your truck?" Jeff checked the bookshelf and the other tables in the room.

"It's not in the truck. I walked home last night."
Lin's face was creased with annoyance. "Maybe I
took it into the room I use for an office." She
hurried in there and looked around. She came out
empty handed.

"How about the kitchen?" Jeff suggested.

Lin and Jeff looked in cabinets, on the floor, on
the table, and around the countertops.

"I'm sure I brought it home." Lin breathed out
an exasperated sigh.

"Well, it will turn up." Jeff gave Lin's shoulder a
squeeze. "Let's go clear the table. I'd better head
home. That alarm is going to go off tomorrow
morning and I'll sleep right through it."

The two went to the deck and gathered the
dishes, glasses, and cutlery and brought it all inside
and loaded the dishwasher. When they finished,
Lin walked Jeff to the front door. Nicky roused
from his blanket and stumbled over to rub his head
against the man's knee. Jeff bent and scratched the
dog's ears. "See you later, little guy."

"Thanks for picking up the dinner." Lin stood
inside the front door.

On the front landing, Jeff shuffled from foot to
foot. When he made eye contact with Lin, her
muscles tingled and she felt all soft and weak.
Electricity jumped between the two of them. For a
second, Lin thought the handsome man would lean
in for a kiss, but he hesitated and the moment was
gone.

"Um." Jeff looked unsure. "Would you like to get dinner with me in town some night?"

Warmth spread through Lin's body. She couldn't believe he was asking her out. Her eyes beamed at him. "Yes. I'd love to."

Jeff breathed a sigh of relief, nodded, and gave Lin a dopey smile. "I have your number. I'll give you a call." As he made his way to his truck, he walked with a spring in his step.

Lin closed and locked the front door and leaned against it with a wide grin on her face. Her heart was beating fast. She hadn't felt so happy in a very long time.

Crossing the living room to go to the kitchen, Lin looked out of the glass door to the deck and noticed something they'd left on the outside table. She opened the door and went out to retrieve it.

Reaching for the object, a shudder ran down her back when she saw what it was. The book she and Jeff had searched the house for was lying on the table, open to chapter eleven.

CHAPTER 12

Lin flung the front door open with shaking hands and Viv hurried in from the dark night pulling her sweater around her. "How on earth did this happen?"

"We searched the house for that book and then it showed up on the table right where we had eaten dinner. It wasn't there when we were eating." Lin's face was pale and her movements were quick and twitchy.

The girls walked into the kitchen and Lin put the tea kettle on to boil water. When she turned back to her cousin, Viv had an odd look on her face.

"What?" Lin's eyes widened.

"You know very well how the book must have gotten out there." Viv had her arms wrapped around herself.

Lin let out a groan. "I know. It's so annoying having a ghost manipulating things. I don't like thinking some stupid ghost is in here spying on me."

"Whoa." Viv hunched over and took quick

glances over her shoulder. "Jeez, don't make him angry. What if he gets angry?"

"The real question is, why not just come out and tell me what he needs to say. Why all this cloak and dagger nonsense?"

"Oh." Viv looked faint. She sat down on one of the counter stools. "Don't say dagger. Hammond was stabbed. Maybe you need to use a more respectful tone when speaking about the ghost." She swallowed. "Have you seen anyone ... ah, floating around in here lately?"

Lin removed the kettle and poured water into the two mugs. "I wish I had. I would give him a piece of my mind."

"Can ghosts hear what you're saying?" Viv asked nervously. Her eyes darted around the room.

Lin placed a mug in front of her cousin and sat down next to her. "I have no idea."

Viv wrapped her hands around the warm mug. "Did you look at the book yet?"

Lin shook her head. Wearily she stood and moved to the side counter where she picked up the *Ghost Mysteries of Nantucket* and carried it back to the center island.

Viv started flipping through the pages. "Hmm. This seems like silly ghost stories. I didn't think an historian like Anton Wilson would write about such things."

Lin leaned over her cousin's shoulder. "Well, I guess the ghost stuff is sort of weaved in with historical information about the island and the inhabitants. Fairytales, ghost stories, legends, they all lend insight into a culture and what's important to the people. Readers can believe the ghost stories if they want to or not."

"You're right." Viv slowly turned some pages. "Which chapter was it opened to?"

"Eleven." Lin sighed. "You look at it. Tell me what it's about. I'm exhausted." She rested her arms on the counter. She wanted to place her head on top of her arms and close her eyes for a minute, but she knew she would doze off if she did. While Viv was reading quietly, Lin was having trouble keeping her eyes open.

"This story is about the mansion behind my house." Viv's excitement shook Lin from her near-doze.

"What's it about?" Lin blinked.

"It's telling about a ghost who lived there. Every day at the same time, a door from a room the family was using as a den would open. Anyone standing nearby would feel an incredible sense of cold. Some members of the family would see a glowing figure in a long dress move out of the room, float along the hallway and head up the stairs. The owners had an alarm system in the house and at that same time every day, the alarm would go off." Viv continued reading. "The family had to have the alarm disarmed." She turned to Lin. "That happened in my house. Remember? Every evening at the same time the alarm would go off. I had the electrician come out several times to check it. He could never figure out what the cause was, so I had him disarm it." Viv's cheeks were pink with excitement.

"So what does it mean?" Lin stared at her cousin. "The ghost from the house behind yours moved into your house?"

Viv's mouth hung open. "Is there a ghost in my house?"

"Would a ghost in your house make Greg Hammond want to buy it? There must be a lot of houses on the island that have a ghost in them. Why would this ghost be so important?"

Viv narrowed her eyes and whispered. "Have you ever seen a ghost in my house?"

"No. Never." Lin shook her head.

"Really? You're not keeping that information from me because you know I'll freak out?"

"I haven't seen anything in there. I swear." Lin held her hand up as if she were taking an oath. She didn't want to tell her cousin that sometimes she had the sensation of a presence or some unusual movement in the old Cape. "Who is the ghost supposed to be? Does the book mention a name?"

Viv bent over and scanned the pages silently. A minute passed and then she let out a gasp.

"What? What is it?"

"The people thought the female ghost in their house was a Witchard and the male ghost was her husband, a Coffin. They owned my house *and* the house behind mine."

"We don't know much about the Witchards." Lin pulled the book closer so they both could see the pages. "Homeowners speculate that the ghosts were Emily Witchard and her husband Sebastian Coffin." Her eyes went wide. "My ghost must be Sebastian Coffin. Our ancestor. But why? What does he want?" Lin read more about Coffin and Emily Witchard. "The book doesn't give much information about them." Lin looked up from the page and blinked. "Anton Wilson. He must know all about the Witchards and Coffins. I'm doing his garden tomorrow." She turned to her cousin. "He told me that the next time I worked in his yard I should stay and he'd show me my family trees."

Viv's voice shook. "Do you think it's safe to be with Wilson alone? Remember Nate Johnson said he saw Anton Wilson near Greg Hammond's boat right before the murder took place. What if...?"

Lin's face took on a serious expression. "When I talk to him, maybe I can find out what he was doing on the docks that morning."

"You need to keep safe. Listen to your intuition. Leave his house if you feel something is off."

Lin said, "I'll be careful."

"Wait." Viv looked worried. "Will you be done with Wilson in time to get to my house? You're supposed to let the workman in to do the repair on the wall near the fireplace."

"Don't worry. I'll be sure to be there to let him

in."

Viv leaned closer. She had a twinkle in her eye and a wicked grin on her face. "So enough about ghosts and murder, tell me all about your good-looking carpenter and how he happened to end up having dinner here with you tonight."

That particular topic took a good hour to discuss and it was well past one in the morning when Viv left for home and Lin stumbled into bed. Before turning out the light, she glared at the alarm clock sitting patiently on the side table right next to the bed.

CHAPTER 13

Anton Wilson yanked open his front door and flew outside when he saw Lin's truck pull up and park at the curb. He crossed the small front lawn and was nearly breathless when he reached Lin's vehicle.

"I was hoping it was you." Wilson's eyes flashed with excitement. "I couldn't remember if today was gardening day or not."

Lin lifted her garden bag of tools out of the truck bed and Nicky, eyeing the animated man, stayed close to her leg. She was wary of the historian and had to force a smile. "Last stop of the day." She'd decided to keep her tools close at hand at all times so that if Wilson threatened her she would be able to fight back. She took a deep breath. When Lin bought the business, she sure didn't think she might have to defend herself against one of her clients.

Following the winding path set between flowering hydrangea bushes, Wilson led the way along the side of the house to the rear gardens. "You'll be able to stay after you finish the work?"

Lin nodded. "I have a bit of time. I have to be somewhere in an hour and half though."

Wilson clapped his bony hands together. "It won't be enough time, but it's certainly a start. I'll go gather the books and folders. Just knock on the kitchen door when you're ready." He hustled off into the house.

Watching him go, Lin was surprised by the small man's energy. Wilson was so thin that it made him seem weak. He looked like he might blow away in a strong wind, but Lin wondered if his wiry build could provide the strength necessary to stab Greg Hammond to death. She shuddered and pushed the thought from her mind.

When she'd finished the gardening, she washed her hands under the hose and splashed cool water on her face. The dog hadn't budged from her side the entire time she worked. "It's okay, Nick. We can handle him if we have to," Lin whispered. She picked up a weeding tool and stuffed it in her back pocket just in case she had to defend herself.

As she was heading to the house to knock on the door, Wilson opened it. "Why don't you come inside?" He held the door wide open. "We can go over the things at the kitchen table." Wilson gestured to the long, wooden table set in front of the huge brick fireplace. Books and folders and sheets of paper spilled over most of the table's surface.

Lin admired the beautiful restoration of the

space. "It's a lovely room."

"I've been living here for a long time. Every room of the house has been lovingly restored."

Wilson pulled out a chair for Lin and the two sat side by side. He reached for a folder and a book. "I've done exhaustive research on the Coffin and the Witchard families, among others of course." He flipped open the folder to display a meticulous family tree. He pointed. "Here you are. You see, as a direct descendant, you go all the way back to two of the first families that founded Nantucket." Wilson's finger hopscotched over the paper stopping for a moment on one member of the family before jumping to the next, all the way back to the mid-1600s.

The historian moved his finger to the section indicating the 1700s. "But this is where things become interesting. Here is your ancestor, Sebastian Coffin, a businessman and lawyer. He was also a director of a newly-formed bank. He did quite well for himself until the bank was robbed. Thanks to an enemy he gained over a disputed business deal, suspicion fell on Sebastian. Many people in town turned away from him despite the lack of evidence that he had anything to do with the robbery. He was removed from his directorship at the bank and lived his life shunned by many townsfolk. Years later, the real robbers were found, but it was too late for Sebastian's reputation. It is a sad tale of how public opinion can ruin a man's career and life.

"How awful." Lin's face clouded. "I wonder why he didn't leave the island and try to start over somewhere else."

"That remains a mystery." Wilson slid the paper closer to Lin. "You see who Sebastian married?"

Lin read the name. "Emily Witchard."

"You have Witchards and Coffins in your blood." Wilson's eyes were bright. "That is a very powerf ...." The man's voice trailed off and he finished the sentence with a different word. "It's very interesting."

Lin was sure he was going to say "powerful" and she wanted to question him about what he meant, but Wilson reached for a book on the table and opened it to show a drawing of the mansion that Sebastian Coffin had built and where he and his wife had made their home until the bank scandal hit.

"I know that house," Lin said. "It's right behind where my cousin lives."

"Which house does your cousin own?"

Lin told him the address. "The backyard of my cousin's Cape house abuts the property of the mansion that belonged to Sebastian and Emily."

"Well, I was not aware of who presently owns the Cape house. I don't know how that fact eluded me." Wilson's bushy eyebrows scrunched together. "In any case, when Sebastian was removed from the bank position, his income plummeted.

Townspeople wouldn't do business with him, so he had to sell the lovely mansion he'd lived in for years. The parcel of land the mansion sat on was quite large, so he had it subdivided and had the smaller Cape house built behind his former home. He and Emily moved there and lived in that house until they passed away." Wilson made eye contact with Lin. "And this I find fascinating. Sebastian was involved in witchcraft." He watched the young woman's face for her reaction.

Lin kept her expression emotionless. "Witchcraft?"

"In early Colonial America, belief in the supernatural was widespread. For example, poor farmers often invoked charms for a favorable harvest. Rumor was that Sebastian had premonitions of the future. Have you ever noticed the little brick extension on the chimney of your cousin's house?"

Lin blinked trying to recall what Wilson was referring to.

"The extension is made of brick and it stands in the shape of an upside-down horseshoe. Such a thing can be seen here and there on the chimney's of old houses on the island. In fact, the oldest house on Nantucket has one as well. You know the house I mean?"

Lin nodded. She knew the shape from seeing the design on several chimneys, but she didn't recall that Viv's house had a chimney with the same design.

"The symbol is supposed to ward off evil and keep witches away." Wilson leaned nearer to Lin, his voice taking on a conspiratorial tone. "But, Sebastian and Emily Coffin didn't believe that witches were evil, they believed that powers could be used for good purposes. It is believed that Sebastian and Emily sheltered people who were about to be accused of sorcery, people who ran away from persecution in mainland towns and came to the island seeking safety. The Salem witch trails ended in the late 1600s, but persecution continued in many areas for years after that. When you have the opportunity, take a look at the bricks on your cousin's chimney. The design on that chimney is slightly askew. Sebastian ordered it to be constructed that way as a symbol to those seeking help and sanctuary."

Wilson let out a chuckle and the suddenness of it startled Lin. "How ingenious the man was. He used the very symbol meant to ward off witches in order to draw those persecuted individuals to safety." Wilson shook his head admiringly. "Sebastian was a very clever man. A good man, as well. Before the bank problem, he was considered by the townspeople to be a kind and generous person."

The alarm on Lin's phone sounded and she jumped. "Oh. I have to go. I need to be somewhere to meet a handyman."

Wilson frowned. "There's so much more to tell. You must stay another time."

Lin wanted to share the family trees with Viv. "Could I bring the folder to show my cousin? I know she'd love to see the information about our ancestors."

Wilson looked like he might reply in the negative, so Lin headed him off. "I could return the folder early tomorrow morning."

"I suppose that would be fine, but please do bring it back tomorrow." Wilson's phone buzzed. He reached for it and stood up. "Excuse me. I must take this."

Lin stood and leaned down to scoop up the papers that were on the table. She stuffed them back into the folder. As she was about to close it, something caught her eye under one of the other papers.

She pushed the documents aside to find a piece of paper showing a hand-drawn interior layout of a house, Viv's house. A surge of adrenaline rushed threw Lin's body. She squinted and read what was written in the upper right-hand corner. The address of Viv's house was written under the words, "Vivian Coffin." Scrawled at the bottom of the paper was, "Greg Hammond" and the name of his boat. Lin's heart pounded so hard she thought it would jump from her chest.

She took a quick glance at Wilson before lifting the paper and slipping it into the folder. Wheeling for the kitchen door, she called good-bye to Wilson who was still speaking on the phone.

Wilson claimed he didn't know who owned the Cape house. Why does Anton Wilson have the interior layout of Viv's house? And why does he have Greg Hammond's name and boat information written on that same piece of paper?

With worry and anxiety swirling through her body, Lin jogged to her truck with Nicky at her heels.

CHAPTER 14

Lin parked her truck in front of Viv's house just as the handyman showed up and the two entered the Cape together with Nicky trailing behind them. Queenie sat on the back of the sofa and she gave the man a dirty look. She didn't care to have her early evening nap interrupted.

When the handyman set down his tool chest and started to work, Lin returned to the front yard so that she could look up at the Cape's red brick chimney. She couldn't see any design on the front, so she walked around to the side of the house. There, on the left section of the chimney, was the small upside-down U-shaped design built into the bricks. Lin turned to the street and she could see that the design would be evident to anyone walking along the road who knew to look for it.

"Hello?" The handyman called to Lin from the front door.

Lin's heart skipped a beat. *Now what?* She walked inside. "What is it?

The man gestured to the wall with his hammer.

"There's the small cupboard. Someone closed it up. It was boarded up and plastered over." He pointed to the broken shelves visible next to the fireplace. "The wood rotted and collapsed and that caused the buckling of the wall that the owner noticed. Parts of the shelves gave way."

Lin wondered why someone would close up the cupboard. Since the handyman was about to pull out the remaining boards of the cupboard, she lifted her phone to take a picture to send to Viv. Lin bent to inspect the broken shelves. She craned her neck to look under the boards. She let out a little gasp of surprise. "There are words written under here." Faded handwriting showed on the bottom of the old shelf.

Ours To Thee

"Ours to Thee?" Lin said aloud. The words pricked at Lin's skin like tiny sparks of electricity biting at her.

The handyman put his crowbar on the floor and looked. "Somebody wrote that a heck of a long time ago."

Lin straightened and looked at the man. "How long ago, do you think?"

"Judging by the look and shape of the letters and by the age of the wood, I'd guess a couple hundred years ago, at least. You'd really need a historian to

J.A Whiting

give you a good estimate."

Lin leaned close to the long-forgotten cupboard and looked down inside the wall where part of the wood had fallen. "There's something in here."

The handyman reached his arm inside past the broken shelves. When he removed his limb, his fingers held a small leather pouch which he placed in Lin's hand. "This must have been on the shelf when it gave way and slid down inside the wall space." He smiled. "A gift from the past."

Cool air enveloped Lin and when the pouch touched her skin, her vision dimmed and the room began to spin. Holding tight to the item from the cupboard, she took shaky steps to the sofa and sank onto it.

The man eyed her with concern. "You okay?"

Lin gave a little nod. "I haven't eaten since breakfast. I'm just feeling a little light-headed." She pushed herself up. "I'd better go get a snack."

Lin stumbled into the kitchen and gently set the leather pouch onto the counter. She closed her eyes and rubbed her forehead. Not wanting to open the pouch without her cousin with her, she sent Viv a text urging her to come home as soon as she could get away from the bookstore.

Is the pouch a clue to why Greg Hammond wanted this house so badly?

Lin took a glass of orange juice and a muffin outside to the deck with Queenie and Nicky following her. Lin sat at the table and stared across the small backyard to the high white fence that separated Viv's property from the large house on the next street that Sebastian Coffin and his wife Emily Witchard used to own.

Everything seemed like a messed ball of yarn with the strings wrapped and twisted together. She needed to clear her head if she and Viv were ever going to figure it out.

The metal click of a bicycle chain caused Lin to turn just as Viv parked her bike next to the shed. She dismounted and hurried toward the deck. "What's wrong? Did the handyman find termites or something? Is my house about to collapse?"

Lin couldn't help a smile from forming. "It's nothing like that."

Viv sank onto one of the deck chairs. "Thank heavens." Relief passed over her face, but it was quickly replaced with an expression of concern. She narrowed her eyes and her tone was cautious. "Why did you tell me to come home then?"

Lin took a deep breath and spent the next twenty minutes telling her cousin about their ancestors, the hand-drawn interior layout of Viv's house found in Anton Wilson's possession with Greg Hammond's name written at the bottom of it, the living room cupboard with a message scrawled under one of the shelves, and the pouch that was found inside the old cupboard. Each new revelation caused a gasp to slip from Viv's throat and when Lin was done relaying the latest discoveries, Viv's cheeks were as red as cherries.

"What does it all mean? I can't even process all of this." Viv's hands gripped the sides of her head. "Why would Anton Wilson have the layout of my house? My name was written on the paper, but he claims not to know who owns the house now? Is he going to break in?" Viv's face went from red to pale in a single beat. "Was he working with Greg Hammond? Did they have a disagreement? Did Wilson murder Hammond because of my house?"

Lin shrugged and lifted her hands in a helpless gesture. "My head is spinning. We need time to go through all the things we know." She tried to gauge her cousin's level of distress. "Do you want to see the leather pouch or do you want to wait and see it later?"

Viv swallowed hard. "Can you go get it? All my energy is drained. If I get up, I'll fall down."

Lin didn't doubt the statement. "It's in the kitchen." She went inside and as she lifted the item from the counter, her fingers received little jolts of energy. Carrying it outside, she placed the pouch on the table in front of her cousin. Viv's face softened when she saw it and she reached out and ran her finger over the little treasure.

"From so long ago. Our ancestors held this."

The two girls just stared at the item for a minute.

Lin said, "It feels like there's something in the pouch."

"Open it," Viv said.

"You should open it." Lin gave the leather pouch a tiny push with her finger so that it slid closer to Viv. "It was found in your house."

"But the house belonged to our grandmother and our great, great, great ancestors. The pouch belongs to both of us." Viv eyed the item. "Anyway, I'm afraid to open it."

Lin tried to ease Viv's concern. "It's probably only some coins or something."

"It's the *or something* part that worries me." Viv gestured and nodded for Lin to do the honors, so Lin reached for the pouch.

"Okay." She put her index finger inside the opening at the top and pressed to nudge the material to move along the two tiny drawstrings that had been pulled to keep it closed. She tipped the pouch and a metal skeleton key slid onto the table with a clunk.

The cousins' eyes widened. Lin lifted the key and the now-familiar jolt of electricity bit at her fingers. She inspected the old metal object and then passed it to Viv who held it gingerly for only a second and then laid it back on the tabletop.

The cousins made eye contact.

"What does it open?" Viv whispered.

"That is a very good question."

The girls heard soft footsteps approaching from the driveway and turned to see Libby Hartnett walking around the corner of the house. She wore a crisp white blouse and softly flowing caramel colored slacks.

"Libby." Viv stood up, surprised to see her regular early-morning bookstore-café customer.

"Hello, Viv." Libby nodded. "Carolin." She stepped up the stairs of the deck. "Sorry to interrupt. I was about to ring the front doorbell, but I could hear the sounds of a saw inside the house and was afraid no one would hear me if I rang, so I came around back."

"Would you like to sit down? Have something to drink?" Viv had no idea why Libby would come for a visit. "Is everything okay?"

The older woman remained standing. "I can't stay. I was walking home from town and passed by your house. I saw Carolin's truck parked at the curb." Libby placed a folder on the table. "I noticed this on the grass next to your truck." She made eye contact with Lin. "I assumed the folder must have fallen from the cab when you got out."

Lin was horrified to think she'd nearly lost Anton Wilson's folder of information and she thanked the woman profusely.

For several seconds, Libby's eyes lingered over the leather pouch on the table and then she said, "I must be on my way. I'll see you at the bookstore in the morning." Libby smiled and walked down the steps.

"Thank you again." Lin called after her.

As she was heading around the corner of the house, Libby looked over her shoulder at Lin with a serious expression. "One must be very careful with sensitive information like that. You don't want it to fall into the wrong hands."

A cold breeze rushed over Lin's skin and was gone as soon as Libby disappeared around the corner.

CHAPTER 15

The overcast morning was a pleasant respite from the week of hot, sunny weather and Lin hoped the cloud cover would remain for the day to keep the temperature a bit cooler. Before heading off to the first gardening job of the day, she drove to Anton Wilson's house to drop off the family tree papers she'd borrowed in order to show Viv. She conveniently did not return the interior layout drawing of Viv's house with the other information contained in the folder.

Just as her finger was about to push on the doorbell button, the door flew open causing Lin to let out a little gasp of surprise.

"You're bright and early. Come in. Have a coffee? Some breakfast?" Wilson had an apron slipped over his head and tied behind his back. The smell of bacon floated on the air and Lin's stomach growled.

"I don't have time really. I just wanted to return the folder."

"Oh, nonsense. A quick coffee and a muffin."

Wilson took the folder from Lin and turned for the kitchen. "Did your cousin enjoy seeing the family trees?"

"She did." Lin followed the man into the kitchen where he poured her a steaming cup and indicated the sugar bowl and creamer. "We'd like to find out more about our ancestors. Viv would like to meet you someday."

"That would be very nice." Wilson set a blueberry muffin on a white plate and placed it in front of Lin. He turned the bacon over on the griddle and poured an egg mixture into the pan set on the stove burner.

"Do you always make a big breakfast?" She bit into the muffin packed with huge berries. Lin wondered if Wilson had noticed that the interior drawing of Viv's house was missing from the folder.

Wilson used a fork to swirl the eggs in the pan. "It is the most important meal of the day, you know."

Lin decided to ask the man some questions. "Did you know the man who was killed down at the docks? Greg Hammond?" Since Greg's name was written on the paper Lin removed from Wilson's kitchen table, she wondered how he would reply.

Wilson eyed Lin as he stirred the egg mixture. "I was familiar with him. I don't believe we'd ever spoken though."

"What do you think happened?"

"Someone wanted him dead." Wilson scooped

the eggs onto two plates. He placed one in front of Lin who was about to protest, but the man said, "You need your strength. You have a demanding job."

Lin couldn't resist the smell so she picked up the fork and dug into the eggs, hoping Wilson hadn't poisoned them. "Did you know anything about Hammond? Why would someone want him dead?"

Wilson used tongs to remove the bacon onto a plate. His jaw set and he paused with the tongs suspended in the air. "Hammond was an unscrupulous man. He played a dangerous game."

A shiver ran down Lin's back. "What sort of game?" She laid the fork across the top of her plate.

"A game he had no business sticking his nose into." Wilson returned to his task.

Lin's eyes were wide. "What sort of game," she asked again, her voice soft.

Wilson seemed to shake himself. "I am engaging in something I find distasteful. Gossip. I really didn't know the man at all."

Lin thought that Wilson seemed to know *something* about Greg Hammond. "You were on the docks the morning Hammond was killed? With Libby Hartnett?"

Wilson slowly raised his eyes and gave Lin a piercing look. "Mrs. Hartnett and I were visiting someone on the docks that morning, yes. Were you there as well?"

"No." Lin shook her head. "I just heard some

114

people talking about who may have heard something that day." Her heart was pounding. She stood up from her seat next to the counter. "Did you hear anything when you were near Hammond's boat?"

Wilson's eyes were like pools of black ice. "Only the sound of the cool breeze rustling past."

Lin's heart thumped. "I'd better get to work." She sidled around the historian and made her way to the front door. "Thank you for the breakfast."

***

Still unsettled by her interaction with Anton Wilson, Lin pulled up to the home of her first client and saw a large white truck at the curb. Driving around to park in front of it, she saw "Hammond Landscaping and Design Services" written in black letters on the side of the vehicle. Wondering why someone from the landscaping company was at the house, Lin and her dog got out and walked past the truck. Scuba equipment lay tossed in the back bed.

At the rear of the home's expansive property, Lin saw Bill, the manager she'd met at Hammond's company who said he hoped to buy Greg's business. He was standing next to the owner of the house. The two were going over some blueprints that Lin assumed must be plans for the back garden.

Carrying her gardening tool bag, Lin approached and called out a greeting.

Bill recognized her. "Oh, hi."

The owner said a quick hello to Lin and then excused himself to go into the house.

"You're doing some work here?" A shiver of unease slid over Lin's skin when she saw creepy Leonard holding a notebook and a heavy measuring tape emerge from behind some tall ornamental grasses growing along a section of the lawn. He leered at Lin and gave her a crooked grin, before moving away to the other side of the property.

"We're putting in stonework here for a patio." Bill moved his arm in the air to indicate the shape. "A fire pit will be there and a pool and hot tub are going in on that side. We'll be doing the stone pathways and area around the water features." The man held out the paper with the design so Lin could look it over. He pointed. "There will be decorative lighting in these areas to enhance the evening experience."

"It's beautiful." Lin tilted her head to the side. "How are things going? Have you completed the purchase of the business?"

"Nearly. It's been pretty straightforward. I'm going ahead and lining up projects now." Bill rolled up the design sketches. "You've been hired to take care of the gardens here?"

Lin nodded. "I bought a small gardening business before I came back to the island. It must be expensive to buy Hammond's company, what with all that heavy equipment and the inventory."

Bill chuckled. "I'd say so. I've been saving for a long time to have my own business. With Greg's business up for sale, I decided to make a bid for his company instead of starting my own. Everything's in place, so it makes the whole thing easier."

Lin sighed. "Did you know Greg well? Did he have enemies?"

Bill's eyebrows went up. "Not to my knowledge."

"I just wonder what happened." Lin gave a shrug. "You worked closely with him. Did he seem worried about anything? Distracted by something? Did he have financial problems?"

"We were just two guys working together. He didn't confide in me. He seemed his normal self." Bill packed the plans away in his briefcase. "Why so much interest?"

"It's sad, that's all. He was a fairly young guy. Cut down in his prime." Lin made eye contact with Bill and he shifted his gaze away. She said, "You never know what can happen, I guess."

"Guess not." Bill picked up his briefcase.

"Do you scuba dive?"

The man gave her a strange look. "What? Why?"

"I saw some equipment in the back of your truck. Did you dive with Greg? I heard he liked to dive, that he liked to treasure hunt."

Bill's face hardened. "Where'd you hear that?"

"Just from people talking."

"We went diving a few times. Greg enjoyed it.

He went a lot. I didn't know Greg to hunt for treasure, though." Bill scoffed. "Someone you've been talking to believes in silly stories." He looked across the yard. "Leonard. You about finished?"

Leonard nodded and headed toward Bill.

Nicky gave a low whine. When Lin turned her head in Leonard's direction, a wave of chilled air hit her in the face and she saw the ghost standing expressionless at the corner of the patio. Lin had to stifle a yip of surprise and she quickly shifted her eyes away from the spirit.

"I better get to work," Lin said. "Nice to see you." She moved to the gardens closest to the house and started to weed and deadhead the flowers. Without looking up, she could feel Leonard's foul gaze on her back as the two men left the property and headed off to the front of the house to their truck.

After thirty minutes of weeding, Lin stood and stretched her back muscles. A whoosh of cold hit her like the blast of frigid air when a walk-in freezer opens. She slowly turned around to see the eighteenth-century ghost standing about forty feet away from her.

Lin rubbed her hands on her shorts. "You should show up when it's ninety degrees outside and I'm dying from the heat." She bit her lower lip worried that using the word "dying" might offend the ghost, but he stood stoically staring at her just as he always did. "The cold breeze I get from you would be great on those hot days."

Lin pulled on the hose and turned the handle on the water faucet. "Don't you get uncomfortably warm wearing that jacket and starched shirt?" She pressed the handle on the hose sending a stream of water into the flower bed. "It would be nice not to have to talk to myself when you're around." She gave the ghost a quick look. "It would also be helpful if you could tell me what's on your mind."

The ghost stood quietly watching Lin work.

She put the hose on the ground. "My cousin Viv says I should ask you questions." She turned and faced the apparition. "You're Sebastian Coffin, aren't you?"

The spirit held Lin's eyes for a single second before becoming more and more transparent until he was gone.

Lin harrumphed and reached for the hose. "I'll be sure to tell Viv that her idea didn't work."

CHAPTER 16

After a long day of gardening, Lin went home and showered and then she and Nicky walked to Viv's house for dinner. Viv was bustling about in the kitchen when Lin walked in through the back door. The little dog greeted Viv and then darted into the living room to find Queenie.

Viv poured seltzer into a glass, garnished it with a slice of lime, and set it in front of the worn out young woman. "You look beat, but at least you're clean."

"I stopped home to shower and change first." Lin yawned. "I thought I'd get used to the hard work by now." She tipped the cold beverage to her lips and swallowed. "So did you talk to Libby this morning? Did you ask her what she meant the other day when she said that we shouldn't let things get into the wrong hands? Did you ask what she was doing with Anton Wilson down on the docks the day of the murder?"

Viv looked sheepish. "I couldn't get the nerve to ask her."

"Viv." Lin used a scolding tone.

"There were people all around this morning. I just never got the opportunity to question her without lots of other ears listening in."

Lin's forehead creased. "When she talked about the folder, do you think she was warning us not to interfere with something or was she trying to be helpful to us?"

"My first instinct was that she was being helpful."

"But?"

"But maybe she wasn't."

Lin groaned. "What's Libby's connection to Anton Wilson?"

"I have no idea. He only rarely comes into the store. I've never seen them together."

"Well, they were together the morning that Hammond was murdered." Lin let out a long sigh. "And Wilson didn't seem to like me questioning him about it." She swirled the seltzer in her glass. "We need to talk to Libby. Do you know where she lives?"

"I know the neighborhood, but not the house. She works part time at one of the specialty shops in town. We could walk over there and see if she's working. Dinner won't be ready for an hour. Want to go now?" Viv looked like she hoped Lin would say they should visit the shop another time.

"Okay." Lin drained her glass. "We also need to check out the attic. We can't keep putting that off.

We need to find out what the key from the cupboard opens."

Viv turned the oven temperature down in case she and Lin were out longer than an hour. "Whatever that key opened is probably long gone by now."

The girls left the house and headed down the brick sidewalks into the center of town where they branched off to one of the side streets. Passing a clothing shop and a bakery, they approached a specialty home décor store.

"I didn't know this place was here." Lin looked in the display windows on the way to the front door.

"It's just as well. We can't afford anything in here anyway." Viv stepped inside with Lin following and the two pretended to browse the aisles and shelves.

A voice spoke behind them. "Hello, girls. You found the store, I see." Libby folded some expensive linen pillow cases and placed them on a shelf.

Lin's throat tightened. *Was Libby expecting us?*

"We're out walking around town until our dinner is ready." Viv smiled. She waited for Lin to handle the questioning.

"Did you keep those papers safe?" Libby made eye contact with Lin as she reached for another pillow case.

"I did." Lin nodded. Her insides fluttered with unease. "This is a lovely store." She tried to make small talk, but thought her voice sounded overly enthusiastic.

"Oh, yes. They carry beautiful things here. I think most people love to surround themselves with luxurious items and here it's possible to pick up a few pretty things as a treat." Libby finished stocking the shelf. "Is there something in particular you're looking for?"

Lin wanted to say "Hammond's killer," but she just shook her head. "We're just looking around."

The three chatted for several minutes, and then Lin asked as innocently as she could, "Have you heard any news about the murder at the docks?"

Libby frowned. "There hasn't been much in the news."

"Are the townspeople talking about it? Does anyone have a guess as to what might have happened?" Lin was working up the courage to ask Libby why she was at the docks that morning.

"People are just making idle speculation, but no one knows anything." Libby moved to a wooden case that displayed blue and white pottery.

Lin followed the woman. "Anton Wilson told me he was at the docks with you that morning."

"Did he? And what did he say we were doing?" Libby arranged the display of pottery pieces that had been moved around by some of the customers.

"Visiting someone."

The corners of Libby's mouth turned up slightly. "Who did he say we were visiting?"

"He didn't mention a name." Lin thought that the older woman was toying with her. "Did you happen to hear anything when you were near Hammond's boat that morning?"

"Just the sound of the cool breeze rushing past." Libby smiled sweetly.

Those words are similar to how Anton Wilson answered that question. Now Lin was sure that Libby was toying with her and her blood started to boil. "I don't think a murder is something to joke about."

Viv's eyebrows went up wondering why her cousin seemed so annoyed.

"Neither do I." Libby's face was serious. "I certainly wouldn't joke about someone's death." She stepped closer and lowered her voice. "Things aren't always as they seem, Carolin."

Lin's mind was racing. *Why did Wilson and Libby give the same answer when she asked them what they heard on the morning of the murder? Did they plan their responses? If they did, why did they?* Lin was so confused that she didn't know what to ask. "I need some air." She turned quickly and strode to the door. Once outside, she sucked in a deep breath.

A man's voice spoke behind her and Lin jumped.

"Hey there, Missy." Creepy Leonard from Hammond Landscaping stood a foot away from her. An unpleasant odor like he hadn't showered in days emanated from the man. His greasy hair hung over his dark, beady eyes. Lin's breath caught in her throat and she had to steel herself to keep from recoiling.

Leonard took a step closer. "I been lookin'...."

Just then, Viv stepped out from the store's front door. Leonard flicked his eyes to her, hesitated, and shuffled away without finishing his sentence. "Have a nice night," he mumbled.

Relief washed over Lin as she watched the man move away from them.

Viv frowned. "Who was that? What did he want?"

Lin told her where she'd met Leonard. "He makes my skin crawl." She linked her arm through her cousin's and they walked along the streets heading back to Viv's house. Forgetting about running into Leonard, Lin ranted about what was going on. "Wilson and Libby both used the very same phrase when I asked them about that morning on the docks ... 'just the sound of the cool breeze.' What does that even mean? Did they conspire to use the same sentence? If they did, why would they do that? Did they have something to do with Hammond's death? They say things, but I feel like their words mean something else."

Lin stopped short.

"What?" Viv asked, cocking her head.

"Something flickered in my mind." Lin blinked. "But I lost it."

Viv sighed. "I hate when you do that." She

looked over her shoulder worried that creepy Leonard might be following them. "Let's go." She tugged on her cousin's arm.

The girls hurriedly walked the final three blocks to Viv's house.

CHAPTER 17

Viv and Lin ate their dinner on the deck. The full moon created a silvery patch of light on the backyard lawn. Nicky darted around the property line sniffing and running under bushes enjoying the pleasantly cool evening air.

"That dog is nuts." Viv sipped from her glass of lemonade.

"The heat knocks him out so when the temperature drops he gets a burst of energy." Lin raised a forkful of chicken marsala to her mouth. "This is delicious, by the way."

When the main dish was finished, the girls nibbled on cookies dusted with confectioner's sugar and spread on top with dark chocolate.

"I can't get Libby and Anton Wilson out of my head." Lin sighed. "Not being able to understand them and how they're connected to the murder, or not, is driving me crazy."

"Give it a rest. You've been thinking too hard. You need to give your brain a break." Viv reached for another cookie. "I'm worried that no one has been arrested. I'm afraid the police will talk to me again and suspect me of the murder."

Lin's heart fluttered with worry. It wasn't possible that the police could arrest Viv. Could they? "Let's get these dishes cleaned up. We need to try and find out what the antique key from the cupboard opens." She leveled her eyes at her cousin. "We're going up to the attic. If you don't want to go, then I'll go by myself."

After cleaning the pans and loading the dishwasher, the girls climbed the staircase to the second floor and entered the larger of the two bedrooms. "That's the door to the attic." Viv pointed to a small door on one of the walls. "The ceiling is slanted so you have to hunch over."

"You mean *we* have to hunch over." Lin reached for the latch and pulled the door open. She knelt down and peered inside. Queenie and Nicky sat beside her eager to see what would happen. "Is there a light?"

"There's a bulb hanging from the ceiling. There's a long string. It's just inside the door on the left."

Lin leaned in and flapped her hand around until she felt the thin string. "I've got it." The light flicked on. "There's a lot of stuff. Do you know what's up here?"

"No." Viv had her arms wrapped around herself. "And I don't want to know."

"I'm going in." Lin scooted into the attic space

waddling like a duck. She moved forward and stood up as much as the ceiling would allow.

"I'm waiting out here." Viv sat down on the bed.

"I don't know what you're afraid of." Lin called from inside the cramped space.

"For one thing, I dislike small spaces. Number two, it's full of cobwebs. Three." Viv paused. "I can't remember the third reason."

Lin ignored her. "There's some old furniture. A rocker. A dresser." Lin tried the drawers to see if any had keyholes in them. "These don't lock though." She shuffled further into the attic calling out the items she came across. "Nothing has a keyhole." Lin's tone was exasperated.

She continued to edge around the attic space checking the items that had been stored trying to find something that required a key to open it, but she came up empty. Her lower back ached from the hunched position she had to maintain. "I'm coming out." She scooted to the door and edged into the bedroom being careful not to hit her head on the low doorframe.

The bedroom light was off. Viv was still sitting on the bed, but her straight posture seemed slightly stiff. Her head was turned away from the attic door towards the open window. Queenie was perched on the sill and Nicky sat next to Viv on the bed, his head facing the window.

"Viv?" Lin stood up.

Viv wagged her hand in the air gesturing for her

cousin to stay back. "Don't come close unless you scrunch down," she whispered. "I turned off the bedroom light so I could see better."

"What's going on?" Lin kept her voice down. She slowly advanced to where Viv sat on the bed in the dark.

"I glanced out the window and some movement caught my eye. I think someone is down there slinking along the bushes."

Lin's throat tightened. "Could it be your neighbor?"

"It's definitely not my neighbor."

"Where is he? Can you still see him?" Lin attempted to move nearer to the window but was impeded by her cousin grabbing the back of her T-shirt.

"Whoever it is will see you if you get too close," Viv warned.

"If one of us doesn't get closer, we won't get a good look at whoever is out there." Lin slid across the wide pine floorboards on her hands and knees. Slowly she rose up so her head was next to the side of the window. She squinted. "I see him. At least, I think it's a him. He's walking around the shed."

Nicky whined and Queenie gave a low growl.

Lin could hear her cousin suck in a breath. Viv asked, "Should we call the police? Is he going to steal my bike?"

"Maybe we shouldn't call the police since they've questioned you about the murder. You don't need their attention on you. Anyway, I don't get the sense this guy is here to steal your bike."

"What sense do you get from him?"

Lin's eyes widened and she straightened.

"Scrunch down. He'll see you," Viv warned.

"He's behind the shed now. I can't see him and he can't see me. But I do see something else."

Lin's words caused Viv to freeze in her sitting position. She stopped breathing for a few seconds. "Is it a...."

Lin didn't answer.

The eighteenth century ghost stood near the property line staring up at the window at Lin's small oval face peering down at him. His usual translucent appearance was enhanced by the shimmer of moonlight through his body. The thought that the man looked ghostly popped into Lin's head and she rolled her eyes at herself. *He looks ghostly because he's a ghost.*

"It's the ghost, isn't it?" Viv's voice was weak. She sounded like she was going to pass out. "Why is he prowling around my yard?"

"He's not. He's just standing there."

"Well, he *was* prowling around by the bushes."

Lin made a face at her cousin. "Viv, you can't see ghosts. You saw a human out there skulking around. A *live* human."

The ghost turned and looked towards the shed. A scuffling sound could be heard. Lin craned her neck to see. A man, his face shrouded in shadow, emerged from the back of the shed, bent, and pushed through the bushes on the property line where he slipped into the next yard.

Lin made eye contact with the ghost as he faded away. She sat back on the floor. *What was that all about?*

The girls spent ten minutes speculating about the intruder. Lin was about to get up from the floor when the doorbell rang and both girls jumped.

"Who can this be so late at night?" Viv's voice shook as she stood and hurried to where Lin sat on the floor.

Lin looked up at her cousin. "Can you see the front door from any of these upstairs windows?" She stood.

Viv shook her head. "You can't see the front door from up here."

Lin glanced out of the side window to see if the ghost might have reappeared. "Then let's not answer."

The bell rang again. The dog whined.

Viv clutched at her cousin's arm with a trembling hand.

"We don't need to answer." Lin tried to calm Viv. "When we don't respond, the person will leave."

The whites of Viv's eyes were bright in the darkness of the room. Her lip quivered. "What if they're trying to see if anyone is at home and if no one answers, they'll break in?"

Lin let out a long breath. "Then we'll block the bedroom door and call the police." She moved to the threshold of the room so that she could better hear if the front door was being forced open. "Go to the window and watch in case the person moves around to the back of the house."

The girls waited for fifteen minutes. There were no more rings of the bell. They ventured down the staircase and Viv slowly opened the front door with Lin standing right behind her with the fireplace poker held like a baseball bat ready to strike. The dog and cat perched on the staircase ready to spring.

No one was there. The quartet went from room to room looking outside from the windows. They stepped onto the deck to check the rear yard.

Lin lowered the poker. "Maybe it was some drunk leaving town. He got disoriented and thought he knew who lived here. It was probably a mistake that he rang your bell, realized his error, and went on his way."

Viv looked skeptical. "Was that a drunk messing around in the bushes near the shed, too?"

Lin didn't have an answer. She hoped it was the same guy. Just someone who wandered into the yard, confused about where he was due to having too many drinks at a bar in town.

The girls stood quietly for a minute.

"You want to sleep here tonight?" Viv had a hopeful expression on her face.

"Yup." Feeling too jumpy to go home, Lin was grateful for the invitation.

As the girls were about to walk upstairs to make up the bed for Lin, Queenie and Nicky turned around on the staircase and headed back up.

"Our helpers." Lin looked at the animals and smiled.

Exhausted and worried, Lin followed Viv up the stairs, not believing for one second that the prowler was just a drunk from town who stumbled into the wrong yard.

CHAPTER 18

Lin tossed and turned and couldn't sleep so she reached for one of her puzzle books. She tried to work on a crossword, but she couldn't concentrate so she closed the book and returned it to the side table. Moonlight filtered in through the open window and pooled on the floorboards. The sheer curtain rode a puff of night air, floated away from the sill, fluttered, and then rested back against the edge of the window. Lin ran her hand over the sleeping dog's fur. Nicky, stretched out on the double bed, snuggled comfortably next to his owner.

The simple furnishings and the peacefulness of the room soothed Lin's frayed nerves. The events of the past weeks bubbled up in a disorganized and unrelated sequence as she tried to put order to the mess.

She pushed back the sheet, slipped her bare feet over the edge of the bed, and padded to the window. The yard was quiet and still, no one rustled through the bushes at the edge of the

135

property or shuffled around the shed. Lin stared at the old structure at the end of the driveway. She wondered if it was built at the same time the house went up.

After staring at the shed for several minutes, Lin straightened and turned for the bedroom door. The dog lifted its head from its comfortable spot and watched his owner leave the bedroom. He stood up, stretched, and jumped off the bed. Nicky followed Lin down the stairs, through the dark house to the kitchen, and out the back door to the deck.

In her long T-shirt, Lin walked barefoot down the steps and around to the shed. She hopped on one foot when she stepped on a large stone and let out a mild curse. Nicky sniffed around the wooden outbuilding and then headed off to the edge of the lawn.

With just the light of the moon to brighten the backyard, Lin made a careful circle around the shed stopping at the locked door. She lifted the metal padlock and gave it a yank, but it remained in place, solid and strong. There was nothing to indicate that it had been tampered with by the nighttime intruder.

Lin stepped back and eyed the roofline and the construction of the walls. As the dog returned from the far end of the yard, Lin moved forward and placed her palm against the shed door.

A few seconds passed and the skin of her hand

began to tingle, but instead of pulling away, she pressed harder on the rough wood. Zings of electricity danced through her hand and up inside her forearm. She dropped her arm just as a whoosh of cold air blew around her like a blast of winter wind.

Lin could see that the dog was looking behind her. His wagging tail pulsed against the worn grass causing puffs of dirt to rise in the air. Slowly, she turned around fully aware of what she would see.

The ghost stood about ten feet from her, the closest he had ever been. His face was solemn. Lin could see that his long bony nose had a bump near the bridge. "Hello, Sebastian."

The translucent specter lifted his eyes to the young woman's face. As little zaps of energy passed between them, Lin realized that she wasn't uncomfortable anymore and she tried to open her mind to the message the ghost seemed to be trying to send her.

Images from the past danced in her brain, but they were wavy and unfocused. She kept her eyes linked with the ghost and just as things in her mind began to clear, Viv stepped from the back door of the house onto the deck. She flicked the light of a flashlight around the back garden and called for her cousin.

Lin heard the spirit say her name, *Carolin Witchard Coffin*. He raised his arm and pointed across the yard beyond the deck and then whatever the ghost was made of separated into a million silver particles that sparkled and disappeared like the tail end of a firework.

What had passed between them tugged at Lin's heart and for the first time, she was sorry to see him go.

She shook herself and wrapped her arms around her shivering body. "I'm here, Viv. By the shed."

"Are you okay?" Viv's voice shook. "Why are you out here? Did you hear someone in the yard?"

Lin and Nicky climbed the steps to the deck. "I had the urge to come outside."

Viv looked dumbfounded. "It couldn't wait until morning?"

Lin sat on one of the deck chairs. "I was in bed. Ideas were running through my mind." She glanced over her shoulder to the yard. "I got a feeling about the old shed."

Viv sat down. "What kind of a feeling?"

"I thought that what Greg Hammond was looking for was inside that shed. But now, I'm not so sure."

Viv's jaw dropped. She looked wide-eyed at the structure through the darkness. "What could be in there?" Her voice trembled.

Lin didn't answer right away. "I don't know, but when I put my hand on the shed door, I could feel little jolts of electricity. Then the ghost showed up and pointed away from the shed."

Viv's hand flew to her mouth.

"The ghost was trying to tell me something, but it didn't come through."

Looking around the yard, Viv clutched her arms around her. "Is he gone?"

Lin nodded. "Nicky can see him, too."

"Oh." Viv gave the dog a look like she thought he might have come from another world.

"What do you know about the shed?" Lin asked.

"Nothing. It's just a shed. It's been there all my life."

"Was it built around the same time as the house?"

Viv shrugged. "I have no idea. Remember Gram used to refer to it as "the barn."

"Right." Lin stood, picked up the flashlight, and walked back into the yard. She pointed the light all over the shed. "Maybe it was originally a barn? Maybe over the years it was made smaller?" She wandered around the structure checking the construction of the walls and scrutinizing the ground to see if there was any indication that the building was once larger than its present size. After ten minutes, she returned to the deck. "I don't think the shed has our answers." Lin looked at her cousin. "I'm going to search the internet to see if there's any information about the house online." She headed inside with Viv hurrying after her.

"Now? Can't it wait until morning?"

"I also want to search on our family names to see what information is online. Maybe we can find something on one of those sites that track and list people's ancestry. Why didn't I think of this before?" Lin stopped and turned. "I forgot my laptop is at my house."

"Use mine. It's in the dining room." Viv yawned. "I'm going back to bed. I have to get up in two hours for work."

***

Lin was sitting at the kitchen table with her eyes glued to the laptop screen when Viv stumbled downstairs early in the morning. She rubbed her eyes while she put the coffee on. "Did you find anything?"

"Yes." Lin's voice bubbled with excitement. "Most stuff we already knew." The rims of her eyelids were red from staying awake most of the night. "But here's the interesting thing." She pulled up a news article on the screen. "It's a story about an open house that was held at the historical museum last year. There were displays set up explaining the island's history and material set out about the early founders."

Viv settled into a chair cradling her coffee mug.

"In one part of the display, there were letters from Sebastian Coffin written to his brother on the mainland and some notes he had written to his wife."

Viv's forehead creased. "So?"

"So," Lin leaned forward.   "During the open house weekend, those letters were stolen."

"Why would anybody want those old letters?"

Lin closed the laptop and grinned at her cousin. "That is what I intend to find out."

CHAPTER 19

Lin opened the door to the old brick building that housed the historical society and glanced around looking for someone who might help her. A short, older man wearing glasses and carrying several books came around the corner and nodded at the young woman.

"I'm looking for someone I could speak to about some archival documents that went missing from here last year."

The man gazed at Lin over the tops of his glasses. "Are you a reporter?"

"I'm related to Sebastian Coffin and Emily Witchard. I was wondering what was in the old letters and why someone might steal them."

"Come and sit down." The man led Lin to a table at the back of the room near the windows.

"You read about the theft in the news?"

Lin nodded. "I was looking for information about my ancestors and came upon the article. I've just recently moved back to the island."

"The only reason someone would want those

letters would be to sell them to a collector. They really weren't valuable."

"Do you recall what the letters discussed?"

"They were simple correspondence between Sebastian and his brother, Nathaniel. They were written after Sebastian lost his standing in the community." The man raised his eyebrows. "You know the story?"

"I do." Lin nodded.

"Very unfortunate. His reputation was ruined after the robbery."

"I don't understand why he didn't regain his reputation after the real thief was discovered."

"The thief was discovered, as was most of the loot, but many items were not recovered, a substantial amount of money, jewelry. People still believed that Sebastian Coffin was the mastermind behind the heist."

"What do you think?"

The man shook his head. "Well, I suppose anything's possible." He gave a shoulder shrug. "Sebastian was probably accused by someone with whom a business deal soured. Sebastian is the only one who knows the whole truth regarding the robbery."

"Do you recall what was written in the letters that were stolen?"

"Sebastian discussed the routine of his days, what he was reading, how the new house had come out. The letters would really only be of interest to a historian or a descendant." The man got a faraway look in his eyes. "There were some sweet letters to Sebastian's wife professing his love for her and praising her tenderness and devotion to him. Remember, this was after he lost his position and was thought to have been the one behind the bank heist. The unfortunate events did not hurt their love for one another. Who knows? Perhaps the adversity they faced drew them closer together."

Lin thought sadly of the unfair turn that Sebastian and Emily's lives took.

The man smiled. "Sebastian called his wife his "treasure.""

Lin's eyes narrowed. "Did he write that in the letters?"

The man folded his hands together and placed them on the table. "Oh, yes. He mentioned his "treasure" quite often in the letters to his brother."

"Do you recall some of the things he wrote?"

The man thought for a moment. "He mentioned that he'd had a room built in the storage barn for himself as a sort of reading and writing room. A place he would go to contemplate and think." The man chuckled. "He told his brother in one letter that the true treasure of his life, his wife, encouraged him to sit and work among his riches."

Lin's head tilted to the side. "What did he mean by that?"

"I assume the riches of his life were learning, studying, thinking, reading." The man stood up.

"We have one of Sebastian's letters here. It was not displayed the day the things were stolen. It was written to a friend of Sebastian, a Quaker minister who lived on the mainland." He led Lin to a back room full of cabinets. "It can't be removed from here, of course."

Pulling open a long, shallow drawer, the man removed a document that had been enclosed in some sort of protective cover. "Most of it has faded and a good part of the letter has been lost, but you can see here where Sebastian speaks of his wife. This was written shortly after Emily passed away." The man read aloud. "My true treasure has passed from this world, but I will keep her locket beside me, in the place where the riches of our lives remain."

A zing of electricity shot down Lin's spine. She lifted her gaze from the old letter and shifted her eyes about the space wondering if the ghost had made an appearance, but she and the man were the only ones in the room.

"A similar sentence was written in the stolen letter to Sebastian's brother." The man closed the cabinet drawer. "Have you heard the rumor that Sebastian had some pirate treasure hidden in his house?"

"Pirate's treasure?" Lin's eyebrows went up.

"Sebastian had many contacts and interactions with different people. The rumor is that he was once paid for services in the form of pirate's loot."

J.A Whiting

The man smiled. "No valuables have surfaced yet, but that doesn't mean there isn't anything." He paused and gave a shrug of his shoulder. "But I do enjoy old tales and I like to think it's possible."

After several more minutes of conversation, Lin thanked the man for both the information and for his time and she left the building hurrying down the granite steps.

***

Holding her phone to her ear, Lin scurried along the sidewalks of town. "So that must be why Greg Hammond wanted your house so badly. Remember Jeff told me that Hammond loved diving and treasure hunting? Hammond must have thought that Sebastian Coffin had some loot buried somewhere on the property."

The chatter of the bookstore café could be heard in the background before Viv spoke. "Good work. Now we have a pretty good idea why Hammond wanted my house. He must have been sure that Sebastian buried some massive treasure in the shed or the house which is kind of stupid because wouldn't it have been found by now?"

"Who knows? If it was well-hidden, maybe not." Lin laughed. "Maybe you ought to hurry home and start digging."

"I can't believe that Hammond would want to buy my house to get his hands on some imaginary

146

treasure. He must have lost his mind."

"Anyway, it's a possible reason why he was so adamant about getting his hands on your property."

"It isn't the answer to our most pressing question, though. Who killed Greg Hammond and why? Actually if we know *who* did it, I don't really care why they did it." Viv asked Lin to hold on for a second and she could be heard talking to a café customer. When she returned to the conversation she asked, "And another pressing question is who was sneaking around the yard last night?"

Lin sighed. "Only one question per day, please."

Viv had to get back to work so the girls ended their conversation just as Lin turned the corner to Viv's house so she could get Nicky and take him home. Her eyes widened and her heart jumped into her mouth when she spotted two police cars parked at the curb next to her cousin's house. Several police officers clustered near the property boundary between Viv's home and the neighboring house.

A small group of people stood on the opposite side of the road. Lin picked up her pace and as she passed Viv's Cape house, she could see the small faces of Nicky and Queenie in the living room window peering out at the commotion.

Lin joined three of the neighbors. "What's happened?"

A young mom who lived across from Viv looked pale and nervous. "The Walkers." She pointed at the house next to Viv's. "Mr. Walker couldn't sleep last night." She couldn't finish her sentence.

A gray-haired, trim-looking man took up the story. "Andy Walker couldn't sleep. He thought he heard some noise outside. He got up and looked out of the bedroom window, saw what looked like two guys scuffling in the bushes. He came downstairs and looked out the dining room window, but didn't see a thing, everything was quiet, so he went back to bed. Early this morning, he got up and came out to walk along the property line where he thought he saw something last night. He noticed a foot sticking out from under the bushes. When he got closer, he saw a guy under the rose bush."

"His face was bloody," the young mom said. Lin wondered why the woman was able to chime in at that point in the story.

"The guy is dead?" Lin questioned.

"No." The gray-haired man continued. "When Andy turned to go inside to call the police, the guy pulled himself up off the ground, limped across the front lawn and down the street. By the time, the police came, he had disappeared."

Lin's heart pounded. The altercation was what she and Viv had seen and heard last night. Her throat constricted. *Did the injured guy ring their doorbell for help last night?* Lin's head buzzed with guilt. The man must have been under the bushes all night.

A surge of anxiety flooded her body. *Were the*

two guys fighting over what they think was supposed to be hidden on Viv's property?

Lin wanted to stay longer to hear if any more information would come to light, but she was already way behind schedule on her gardening jobs for the day. She jogged to Viv's house to pick up Nicky. When she hurried through the front door, Lin stopped short as an idea flashed in her brain. *What if it wasn't two guys fighting last night? What if it was a guy and a woman?*

Lin called to the dog so that they could hurry home and get the truck. "Come on, Nick. We have an important stop to make."

CHAPTER 20

Lin stopped the truck a block away from her intended destination. She and the dog got out and walked down the street. Lin carried her gardening tool bag in case they were found out and questioned. They stopped one house away from Anton Wilson's home.

"You need to stay quiet." Lin held the dog's eyes. "We need to approach slowly. I don't want anyone inside to see us. We'll go around back and I'll try to peek in some windows. Try to see if Anton Wilson is hurt inside."

The two made their way to the house and slipped around to the back. Just as Lin was about to press her face to one of the windows, a voice spoke behind her and she nearly jumped out of her skin.

"It isn't polite to peer into people's windows, Carolin."

Sweat trickling down her back, Lin turned slowly to see Libby Hartnett standing next to her. Lin babbled. "I rang the bell. No one answered and I...."

Libby's eyes narrowed. "It isn't polite to lie, either."

The two women stared at each other for a few moments, and then Libby sighed and started toward the back door of Wilson's house. "Come inside. There are some things that I need to talk to you about. I hoped to have this conversation later, but you need to know some things."

Lin hesitated. She was about to whirl and run away when Libby said without turning around, "Don't bother to run, Carolin. I'm faster than you."

Anton Wilson was sitting at the kitchen table when the women entered and he jumped up out of his seat. "Carolin." He gave Libby a look of surprise.

Libby waved her hand in the air. "We need to talk to her. She needs to be told some of it."

Anton looked from one to the other. "But...."

"There aren't any buts. Miscommunication is causing problems." Libby sat at the table. She gestured for Lin to sit.

Lin eyed Wilson. "I see you haven't been stabbed."

Wilson's jaw dropped. "What?"

"You don't know? I'm surprised. I thought the two of you knew most everything that went on in town."

"There's no need to be snippy." Libby looked at Lin with kind eyes. The corners of her mouth turned up in a soft smile. "I can see how you might feel distrustful of us, but honestly, we've had your best interests at heart." The woman sighed. "We're thrilled to have you here on the island, Carolin. Truly."

Wilson said, "I hate to interrupt, but what's this business about being stabbed?"

Lin explained about the altercation in the tree line between Viv's property and her neighbor's land. "I thought it might have been you two fighting." She looked at Wilson. "I wondered if you had been stabbed by Libby."

"Why would we be fighting?" Wilson eyed Lin.

"Because you know that there might be something valuable on Viv's land. You must know that I saw the hand-drawn interior of Viv's house that you had." Lin wanted answers. "What do you think is hidden there? Part of the old bank heist from hundreds of years ago?"

Wilson snorted. "That isn't what we care about."

"What *do* you care about?" Lin faced Libby. "And why are you so happy to have me on the island?"

Libby paused for a few beats, and then she reached out her hand to the young woman sitting next to her. "Take my hand."

Lin was about to scoff at the odd request, but something stopped her. Gingerly, she lifted her arm, hesitated for a moment, and then placed her hand on top of the older woman's palm.

A rush of calm and ease flooded Lin's body. She

experienced a feeling of safety, of being protected. A picture formed in her mind and it was like she was watching a movie or was peeking in on someone's life through a window. The edges of the images were ragged and unclear, but she could make out the scene.

The rocking motion of a boat caused her to feel slightly unsteady. A man stood at a small stove moving a fork over something in the frying pan. The smell of onions and garlic reached her nose. Footsteps approached. A man's voice. Angry words. A shout. The thrust of a hand holding something sharp. A grunt. The man falling to the floor.

Lin shuddered and pulled her hand loose from Libby's grasp. "What was that?"

"I'll tell you what you probably saw." Libby recounted the images that had flashed through Lin's brain.

"How?" Lin's eyes were wide. Her hands trembled. She was ready to bolt from the house.

Libby folded her hands in her lap. "You and I are related, although very distantly. We are both descended from the Witchard family. Some of the Witchard women have special gifts. It took us a while to determine if you had skills." Libby made eye contact with Lin. "You're one of us, Carolin. You're not alone. Not anymore."

Lin gaped at the woman. She couldn't believe her ears. There were other people on the island with similar skills to her own? Her heart nearly burst with joy.

"You can see things?" Libby asked cautiously.

Lin swallowed hard. She didn't answer.

Libby phrased her previous question in a different way. "You can see the spirits of those who have passed?"

Lin gave a slight nod. She had never met anyone else who had special skills. Her head was spinning, a million questions swirling in her brain.

"We suspected you could. You feel a cool breeze when a spirit is near?"

"Yes."

"Recently, Anton and I answered a question that you asked us in the same way," Libby said. "We wanted to see your reaction when we mentioned a *cool* breeze was what we heard at the docks. We were trying to determine if you could see the ones who have passed. I sensed that you could." Libby's expression was serious. "It's very powerful to have both Coffins and Witchards in your blood. And to be firstborn magnifies any skills that you have." Libby cocked her head. "You've seen spirits recently?"

"Yes." Lin's voice was soft.

Libby's eyebrows went up, revealing her excitement. "Have they spoken to you?"

"I see the ghost of Sebastian Coffin, when he decides he wants to be seen."

Wilson let out a gasp. His eyes were wide and a

huge grin spread over his face.

"He never speaks. He just looks at me." Lin's forehead creased. "Although, the last time, it seemed that he was trying to communicate something to me, but without using words. It was all fuzzy and I couldn't understand it."

"If it happens again, just let it flow. Don't try too hard," Libby said. "Relax. Just be open to the messages."

"Why am I seeing things now? When I was young, I could always stop it from happening. Now, no matter what I think or try, I can't stop ghosts from appearing."

"I'm not sure I have an answer." Libby leaned slightly forward. "Perhaps if a child says no, then the request is respected, but an adult, well, if a spirit has a message of importance...."

Lin thought about that. It seemed to make sense.

"When I held your hand, could you make out any of the words spoken between the men in the vision?"

"No. I could just hear the voices and the angry tone."

"Did you get a look at the killer's face?"

Lin cringed and shook her head. She wished she could be of more help. She glanced at Wilson and then back at Libby. "Why were you at the docks that day?"

"Every morning, my friends and I meet at your

cousin's bookstore. We heard your cousin and her employee discussing Greg Hammond's harassment. I had a premonition of trouble. Anton and I worked to figure out why Hammond was after that particular house."

"We make a good team." Anton smiled at Libby. "With my historical knowledge and Libby's skills, we've been able to figure some things out."

"Despite Mr. Hammond's desperate pursuit of your cousin's house, I sensed that he was in danger," Libby said. "Anton and I visited the docks that morning. We called on Mr. Hammond at his boat, but he wasn't there. We waited for a short time and then we decided to walk around in the hopes we would run into him." Libby sighed and looked down.

"We were a bit too early." Anton's face was tense. "Mr. Hammond returned to his boat after we had left. Unfortunately, the killer had better timing than we did."

Lin's expression was serious. "Do you know why Hammond wanted Viv's house so badly? Did he think there was something valuable hidden somewhere on the property, maybe money from the supposed involvement in the bank robbery? I heard recently that there was a rumor that Sebastian had some pirate's loot. "

Wilson's eyes widened. "You know that rumor?"

Lin said, "I talked with the man at the historical society."

"I don't believe Sebastian was involved in the bank robbery," Wilson said. "Some people on the island believed that Sebastian and Emily took in people who had run away from the mainland because they were afraid of being accused of witchcraft. Believe it or not, some of those people were very wealthy. Speculation was that Sebastian may have received valuables for helping people escape from persecution. My research indicates that Sebastian and Emily received gifts from the people they helped, some very valuable gifts." Wilson paused. "Have you heard of the pirate, La Buse?"

Lin shook her head.

"La Buse was born in Calais in the late 1600s. He was a naval officer who later became a pirate. He's known for hiding one of the biggest pirate treasures in history. It's never been found. Today the treasure would be worth well over a billion dollars."

Lin's eyes bugged out.

"It is possible that Sebastian received some items thought to be from La Buse's treasure as well as some documents with instructions indicating where the full loot is buried in the Seychelles. Sebastian wrote to his brother about the gifts he'd received saying he felt obligated to accept them, but that he would never sell the items. He did not want to benefit from someone else's misfortune. We assume that Greg Hammond was aware of that information."

"How would Hammond know all of this?" Lin was puzzled.

"I wrote about it in one of my books. A long time ago." Wilson folded his arms over his chest. "If some items of value are hidden on your cousin's property, it would add to the historical record of what we know of Sebastian and Emily Coffin."

Lin was about to ask a question when Libby's phone chimed and the woman stood to take the call. After a few moments, she clicked off. "Anton and I have an appointment we must get to. Can you meet me at the bookstore in the morning so that we can continue our chat?"

Lin agreed and a time was set to gather at the bookstore early the next day.

"We need to figure out who killed Greg Hammond." Libby's face clouded. "There is a dangerous person lurking on our island. He wants what isn't his. He has to be found." The woman put her hand softly on Lin's arm. "If you're willing to help, we can talk tomorrow about how best to join forces. We need you, Carolin." Libby studied Lin's face and smiled. "I can sense your grandfather's love all around you."

Lin's heart swelled and she blinked back tears. She'd finally found someone like her. There was so much to know and discover and she couldn't wait to fire questions at Libby. She could barely squeak out the words from her emotion-filled throat. "I want to help."

Lin and the dog left Wilson's house and headed up the street to her truck. With misty eyes, she looked down at Nicky trotting along beside her. "I'm not alone, Nick. I'm not alone."

CHAPTER 21

Lin stepped out of the front door of Viv's house. "You two behave," Lin told Nicky and Queenie. "And be sure to protect the house." She locked the door and pulled it closed. Lin was heading into town to meet Jeff at a pub for dinner.

Viv and her band had a gig to play at a night-spot down by the docks. Viv's boyfriend was still in Boston so a friend of theirs was sitting in for him on the keyboards. Viv was still uneasy about the evening intruder in her yard, so she asked Lin to stay overnight with her again.

Lin was so excited to see Jeff that she practically skipped down the street, her long brown hair swinging beneath her shoulders. Lin chuckled when she realized this would be the first time he would see her when she wasn't covered in sweat or garden grime so she chose her cutest summer dress to emphasize her nicer appearance.

Jeff was waiting at the pub entrance and when she turned the corner and he caught sight of her, he beamed and strode up the sidewalk to greet her.

"You look great." He gave her a hug and held her hand as they walked the few steps to the pub door. Lin's heart raced and her cheeks tinged with pink.

"I thought maybe you wouldn't recognize me all cleaned up." Lin's blue eyes were shining.

"Well, you did shower the night we got takeout for dinner," Jeff smiled as he reminded her.

They sat down at a table near the window and sipped drinks while perusing the menu. Once they ordered, they chatted about their week and the talk turned again to the murder of Greg Hammond. Lin told Jeff about the bank heist, the notion that Sebastian Coffin helped persecuted people settle on the island, and the rumor that Sebastian and Emily had received valuable items from a pirate's treasure for helping those people live in safety.

Jeff set his beer glass on the table. "Greg would be very interested in that. He probably thought that he'd find the long-lost treasure and all of his problems would be solved." He gave Lin a serious look. "I heard some rumors, too." He seemed reluctant to share.

"What did you hear?"

"I met a couple of friends for lunch the other day. One of them heard something about Greg's company being in financial peril. Greg put the business up for sale right before he was killed. An audit is being done on the company. It's hush-hush. They don't want to tip off any of the employees that there are questions about the finances. It seems someone may have been stealing from the business, probably still is."

Lin straightened. "I'm not surprised. My guess would be Leonard. When I stopped in at the landscape company a while ago, it seemed that Leonard had free rein in that office. He didn't want me in there. He could very well be the one stealing from the company."

Jeff nodded. "If the business was sinking financially, then Greg's desperation to find hidden money in your cousin's house makes a lot of sense."

"But if his finances were a mess, how would a bank ever give him a loan to buy Viv's house?" Lin asked.

"He could have used his business for collateral. It's a big property, a well-known business on the island."

Lin let out a long sigh. "I wish the police would make an arrest. Then Viv wouldn't have to worry about being a suspect. The whole thing is wearing her down."

Jeff reached across the table and took Lin's hand. "I think the whole thing is wearing on you, too."

She gave a reluctant nod and whispered. "You're right. It is. They couldn't pin this on Viv could they?"

The edges of Jeff's mouth turned down. "I hope not."

Thinking about her cousin being falsely accused caused anxiety to pulse through Lin's body.

To lighten the mood, Jeff suggested sharing a dessert and they ordered a slice of key lime pie which arrived on a pale yellow plate with two silver spoons. When the date was over, Lin and Jeff stood on the sidewalk in front of the pub and shared a sweet kiss before parting ways. Despite the late hour, Jeff had promised to help a friend pull out some old kitchen cabinets in preparation for a remodel. He offered to drive Lin to Viv's house, but Lin wanted to go see her cousin's band playing in town.

Lin walked along in the light from the streetlamps and headed to the club where Viv and her band were playing down near the docks. Tourists were out in full force strolling by the stores and pubs and walking along the wharves to look at all the boats. Turning the corner, she noticed that the streetlights were out and that storefronts were dark in this section of town. People spilled onto the sidewalks and Lin heard them discussing the area power outage. Approaching the club, Lin spotted one of Viv's band members amid the crowd at the curb.

"Viv went home. The power went out halfway through our first set. The guys packed up the equipment. I'm just waiting for Joe to come by with the van."

Lin thanked the young woman and turned for

Viv's house. As she walked, she pondered what she'd learned about the case. No one had been arrested yet so Viv was still a possible suspect. Three hundred years ago, Emily and Sebastian Coffin helped people who fled the mainland out of fear of persecution for witchcraft to settle on the island. Emily and Sebastian may have received valuable gifts for their help. Those gifts had never been located and are thought to be hidden on Viv's property. Greg Hammond's business was in financial trouble and he'd put the company up for sale shortly before he was killed. Hammond desperately wanted Viv's house hoping to discover the valuable items which would have solved his financial woes.

Distracted by her thoughts, Lin turned the corner and smacked into a woman carrying two bags of groceries. The bags hit the ground spilling some of the contents out onto the sidewalk. "I'm so sorry." As she was about to kneel to gather the things, Lin recognized the woman as one of her gardening clients. "Oh, Mrs. Abbott. I was so distracted and not paying any attention." She repacked the bags.

The small, silver-haired woman smiled. "It's happened to all of us. Don't worry. Nothing I bought can be hurt in a tumble. The wheel broke on my shopping pull-cart so I had to carry everything."

Lin stood, her arms wrapped around the bags,

all the items safely inside. "Let me carry them for you. I'm heading in the same direction."

Mrs. Abbott gave a meager protest, but it was plain that she was grateful for the help. The two started up the lane heading for Main Street. The woman's small home was tucked a few blocks away on a side road in town. They chatted about Mrs. Abbott's gardens which were full and lush this year and the woman credited Lin's care with their success.

Halfway up the hill, the topic changed. "So terrible about Greg Hammond." Mrs. Abbott tsk-tsked and shook her head. "Such an awful thing. Our island is usually so quiet and peaceful. The poor man. Did you know him?"

Lin shook her head. "I was introduced to him only briefly." She kept Hammond's harassment of Viv to herself.

"He was a nice person."

Lin looked at Mrs. Abbott out of the corner of her eye. That wasn't the way Viv would have described the man. "Was he? You knew him?"

"He put in my garden plants a few years ago and he did the brick walkway recently." The old woman gave a sad sigh. "He'd join me for tea. We had some very nice discussions. We talked about everything, flowers, of course, but current events, books, history, especially the history of the island. He was quite knowledgeable."

"What do you think happened? Was he in

trouble with someone?'

Mrs. Abbott gave a little snort. "Greg was in trouble with himself mostly. Money slipped right through his fingers like water through a sieve. He needed to pay more attention to his company." The woman looked over her shoulder and lowered her voice. "Greg was sure one of the employees was stealing from the business. He was positive that he should have been making more money than he was. He was trying to figure it out."

Lin was shocked that Hammond would confess such things to a customer. "He told you this?"

"Oh, yes. Greg put the business up for sale. He figured an audit right before sale would uncover the wrongdoing."

"Did he tell you who he suspected?"

"No. He didn't want to accuse someone without proof. He came by the day before he was killed to fix the patio. The cold winter weather had forced up some of the bricks. He told me that his fortunes were about to change."

"Did he say how?"

"Greg finally figured out who was stealing from him. He planned to go to the police with the information the very next morning." The woman's face clouded. "He never got there." Mrs. Abbott let out a heavy sigh. "How I wish he'd told me the name of the devil who stole from him so that I could inform the police."

Lin's heart was beating fast as they turned onto

the woman's front walk and then went up the stairs to the porch. Under the porch light, Lin could see a frown pulling on Mrs. Abbott's facial muscles.

"Do you think the embezzler knew Greg was on to him? Do you think he killed Greg?"

"I wouldn't be surprised," the woman said solemnly.

"Did you tell the police about this?" Lin asked.

"Indeed, I did." Mrs. Abbott stood a little straighter. "But no one's been arrested so it mustn't have been any help."

"I bet it was a huge help." Lin's mind was racing. A thought popped into her head and gave her such a jolt that she nearly dropped the grocery bags. "Would you like me to bring these inside?" She wanted to hurry away to pursue her idea.

"No, my dear. Just set them down." Mrs. Abbott pointed to the porch floor and thanked Lin for her help.

Lin was about to hurry down the front steps when Mrs. Abbott let out another sigh as she fumbled in her purse for her house key. "Poor Greg. He really seemed very much alone in the world."

Lin's heart clenched. She stood still for a moment and then she moved slowly down the steps. For a good part of her life, she'd been all too familiar with the feeling of being alone.

CHAPTER 22

Leonard. It had to be him. Lin raced up Main Street to get to Viv's house as fast as she could.

Leonard had access to Hammond's back office files and he was probably in need of money. Greg ignored the business so it must have been fairly easy to doctor the books. He must have known that Greg was interested in Viv's house. He must have seen the books that Greg was reading. Maybe Leonard even knew what Greg hoped to find on Viv's property. Lin's brain was trying to fit all the pieces together. He must have known that Greg had discovered that he was embezzling from the business so, to save his skin, Leonard murdered Greg. Lin berated herself for not seeing it sooner.

A shadow stepped from a dark yard onto the sidewalk in front of Lin causing her to pull to a halt.

Leonard.

Fear gripped her throat and her body felt like rubber. She wanted to whirl and run, but she didn't want to incite him. She forced herself to take slow breaths.

The man's face was bruised and cut. His hair hung in long strings around his cheeks. Leonard's lip was twice its usual size.

He must have been one of the two men fighting at the side of Viv's yard the other night.

"I been lookin' for you." Leonard shuffled to the side so that he wasn't directly under the streetlamp.

Lin glanced around, but there was no one walking in the area. She took a tiny step back. She swallowed hard, but her constricted throat only allowed her voice to come out as a squeak. "What do you want?"

"I need to tell you something." Leonard flicked his eyes side to side and up the street.

"I need to get home." Lin's heart pounded so hard she was sure that her chest would burst open. She took a step to her left, but Leonard moved to block her way.

Even in the thin light of the streetlamp, Lin could make out Leonard's yellow, chipped teeth.

"I'm in trouble," Leonard mumbled.

"Yeah, I know."

Leonard's face screwed up. "How would you know?"

Lin wished she was a foot further back from the man. If she tried to run, he would just reach for her arm and grab her. She waited for an opportunity.

"People talk." Lin forced her shoulders back.

"Nobody knows this." Leonard stepped closer.

Lin gently slid both of her feet an inch out of her

flip flops so that when she got the chance she could more easily step out of them and run as fast as she could.

A car came up the small hill of the street and caught the two people standing on the sidewalk in the headlights. Lin would rather be hit by a car than dragged away and killed by Leonard.

Lin bolted into the road in front of the vehicle hoping they would see her and stop in time to avoid hitting her. She grimaced and closed her eyes waiting for the hit.

Leonard ran into the yard of the house to his left and disappeared into the trees.

The car screeched to a stop. The driver jumped out and hurried to the side of the shaking young woman standing in front of him in the dark.

***

When the police arrived, Lin was still shaken. She explained why she had run into the road. "I think a guy who works for Hammond Landscaping is responsible for killing Greg Hammond. The guy's name is Leonard. I don't know his last name."

The two officers exchanged a look. One of the men said, "We know who you mean. It's not him though."

Lin's eyes flashed. "Why isn't it him?"

The other officer spoke. "We know where Leonard was the morning Mr. Hammond was killed."

A questioning expression spread over Lin's face and she tilted her head to the side. "You do?"

The first officer nodded. "He got into some mischief the night before. He was a guest at the police station until after the murder took place."

Lin's shoulders drooped. She felt foolish for making the accusation.

"Did he threaten you this evening? Do you want to make a formal complaint against Mr. Reed? Leonard Reed."

Lin blinked. "No." She shook her head. She wanted to get away from the police officers and get to Viv's house where she could forget the whole evening. The officers offered to give her a lift, but she declined and instead, walked the remaining few blocks to her cousin's place.

The house was dark when she arrived. She unlocked the front door and flicked on the lights. The dog greeted her with sleepy eyes and Queenie arched her back and yawned from her place on the sofa.

"I made a fool of myself tonight," Lin told the animals. She let out a long groan. She kicked off her flip flops and climbed the staircase to the spare room where she pulled off her dress and put on a T-shirt and a pair of long pajama pants. She picked up one of her crossword puzzle books, went downstairs and into the kitchen.

Nicky woofed to be let outside. Following the

dog to the back door, Lin texted her cousin. A moment later, Viv replied that when she was on her way home after the power outage at the club, she had to stop at the bookstore because an employee was sick and couldn't finish her shift. She'd just finished locking up and would be home in a few minutes.

Lin opened the back door, let the dog out, and stepped onto the deck. Cloud cover hid the moon and stars making the yard unusually dark. She sucked in a long deep breath and sat in one of the chairs.

How could she have been so wrong about the killer? Everything seemed to fit. A wave of guilt washed over her. It had been easy to suspect Leonard. The way he looked and his poor social skills made Lin uncomfortable and she always wanted to get away from him, but those things didn't make him a murderer. She'd been too quick to jump to conclusions.

Lin looked out over the yard. "Nick?" She stood and walked down onto the grass where she called the dog's name again.

Bits and pieces of information flashed in Lin's mind like tiny sparks. Leonard had said that he wanted to tell her something, he'd said he was in trouble. He looked like he'd been in a fight. Other thoughts sparked in her brain and her mouth dropped open in realization.

Just about every time the ghost had appeared,

one particular person was present. Lin closed her eyes. Everything aligned and pointed to one person. *My God. How did I miss it? I know who killed Greg Hammond.*

Nicky's insistent whine from behind the shed shook Lin to attention. A man's moan floated on the air. Flickers of anxiety pulsed down her back as Lin rushed to where the sounds were coming from. Rounding the corner of the shed, Lin saw Nicky standing over a man who lay on the ground face-up.

Lin moved closer. She could see blood on the man's face and chest. *Leonard.* She reached wildly for her phone, but when she shoved her hand into her pajama pocket, it was empty. She let out a curse.

Lin leaned closer to the man and whispered his name. As she reached her hand towards Leonard, cold air surrounded her and something caught her eye to the left.

The ghost. His eyes were wide. With a swoop of his arm, he pointed behind her.

Lin sensed movement. She hit the ground and rolled to the side narrowly missing being struck from behind. Leaping to her feet, she faced Bill Ward. He held a knife in his hand.

"You." Lin sucked in a breath. "You greedy monster."

"Save it." Bill spat out the words and slowly circled preparing to lunge.

Having just arrived home, Viv stepped from the

back door of the house and scanned the yard looking for her cousin. "Lin?"

Lin yelled, never taking her eyes from Bill Ward and his silver knife. "Stay inside, Viv. Call the police. Lock the door."

Bill rushed at Lin holding the knife in his right hand like a spear. Lin side-stepped to her left which made the force of the man's swing less effective, the thrust of the knife less powerful. She brought her right forearm up like a shield. The knife grazed her arm. Lin spun around and using the whole sole of her foot, she kicked Bill in the back of his leg.

Just as the man's knee buckled, Nicky jumped up and chomped into Bill's leg. At the same moment, the dark gray cat leaped through the air from the top of the shed. The snarling feline sank her claws into the man's shoulders and her fangs bit into his neck. Her back legs ripped through the assailant's shirt and into his skin.

Bill screamed and lost his balance. The knife fell from his hand and hit the ground with a thud. While the cat and dog continued their attack, Lin kicked out and the blade scuttled across the lawn out of Bill's reach.

Viv rushed off the deck and into the yard, wielding the fireplace poker like a spear. Her chest heaving, Lin saw her cousin running towards Bill like a banshee. She couldn't help a tiny smile from spreading over her lips.

The letdown from the sudden release of adrenaline in her body caused an enormous flood of fatigue to wash over Lin. Then she burst into tears.

CHAPTER 23

Lin, Jeff, Viv, and John sat in beach chairs overlooking the ocean. Lin pushed her toes under the warm, soft white sand and rested her head against the chair back. The four had spent an hour body-surfing and floating on the waves and were now warming themselves under the late June sun. Viv had packed the cooler with roasted chicken, pasta salad, crusty Italian bread, and yogurt and fruit parfaits layered in little plastic cups. It was a chance for everyone to relax and enjoy the warm, summer day after the strange events of the past few weeks.

"So, fill in the details for us." Jeff sipped from a can of seltzer.

Viv groaned. "I don't want to talk about it anymore. I'm just glad it's over and things can get back to normal."

Lin sat up in her chair and adjusted her sunglasses. "I'll tell you about it. Where should I start?"

"At the beginning." John smiled. "I leave the

island for a week and everything is solved when I get back."

Lin stretched her legs out over the sand. "Bill Ward was stealing from Hammond Landscaping for years. His wife was the bookkeeper and she doctored the stats to make it seem that, over a few years time, the company was sliding into financial trouble."

"How convenient that Bill Ward's wife was a bookkeeper." John shook his head.

Lin continued. "Recently the speed of the embezzling picked up. Hammond was frantic about the rapid loss of money. He'd been reading histories of the island for years and he believed the stories that said Sebastian Coffin had hidden valuables on his property. If Greg could get his hands on those valuables then his financial troubles would have been over."

Viv sighed. "That's when he started his pursuit of my house."

"Leonard told the police that Greg talked to him about his concern that someone in the company was stealing from him," Lin said. "Greg always talked about the island stories and history with Leonard. Leonard thought that looking for pirate's treasure at Viv's house was folly, but he humored Greg."

Even though Viv had said she didn't want to talk about the whole mess, she was drawn into the telling of the story. "Greg told Leonard that he suspected Bill of embezzling. Bill revealed to the police that he'd overheard Greg making accusations against him and that he had no choice but to kill Greg in order to silence him. Bill used his scuba equipment to approach Greg's boat in the water early that morning. That way no one saw him on the docks."

"I'm ashamed that I jumped to the idea that Leonard was the killer." Lin frowned. "He came into town twice to tell me that Bill was stealing and that he'd probably killed Greg. Leonard was trying to do the right thing and I just thought he was harassing me."

Jeff reached over and took Lin's hand.

Viv put on a sun hat. "The night we heard noises outside and saw a man in the bushes, it was Leonard and Bill having a fight. Leonard followed us home from town that evening. He came to the house to try to tell Lin what he knew, but he saw Bill in the yard. Bill was trying to break into the shed to hunt for the valuables Greg claimed were hidden there, but Leonard confronted him about the embezzling and the fight broke out."

"Leonard pulled out a switchblade and Bill took off. Leonard rang the doorbell, but we didn't answer. Turns out, he had a concussion from the fight. He ended up collapsing in the bushes on the edge of Viv's yard."

"Leonard had been hiding out after the fight. He knew Bill would try to kill him. That last evening,

Leonard returned to Viv's house after trying to talk to me on the sidewalk." Lin rubbed her forehead. "Bill had been hunting for Leonard since they fought the day before. Bill tailed him to Viv's and attacked him in the yard. That's when I went outside with the dog and found Leonard hurt behind the shed."

"Lucky the animals were so determined to protect you. They were a big help." Jeff squeezed Lin's hand. "But I think all the bending and squatting you've been doing in the gardens has strengthened your legs and made you quick and that helped you take Bill down."

Lin nodded and then she chuckled thinking of Viv rushing out of the house with the fireplace poker. "Well, if Nicky and Queenie hadn't helped me, Viv would have taken care of Bill Ward single-handedly."

"You bet I would have." Viv flexed her arm to show a muscle.

"Oh, and unfortunately, there was no treasure in the shed," John told Jeff.

"We searched for hours." Viv removed the lunch items from the cooler. "We didn't even find a single coin." Viv served the chicken and pasta on paper plates and passed them around. Everyone dug into the tasty meal and showered Viv with praise for the delicious lunch.

Lin balanced the plate on her lap and sipped from her water bottle. She hadn't been able to shake the feeling that they just hadn't searched in the right place.

***

After returning from the beach, the guys said their goodbyes and headed off. The girls showered and changed into comfortable clothes, made tea, and sat down in the living room. Queenie and Nicky slept peacefully on cushions in the corner of the room.

The bulge in the wall near the fireplace had been repaired and repainted. "The wall looks great," Lin said.

Viv put her legs up on the ottoman. "I'm happy with it. I'd hire that guy again. Hopefully I won't need his skills any time soon."

The sound of a car's engine could be heard in Viv's driveway and a few minutes later the doorbell rang. Libby Hartnett, carrying a bottle of wine and a box of chocolates, and Anton Wilson holding a bouquet of flowers, stood on the front stoop and called greetings to the two young women through the screen door.

"We brought some things to help you recover from the ordeal." Libby placed the wine and sweets on the coffee table in front of Lin.

"And some flowers to brighten the day." Anton placed the vase of blooms on the side table.

Lin thanked them both for their thoughtfulness.

A Haunted Murder

"Please sit." Viv invited Libby and Anton to join them in having a mug of tea and they accepted.

When everyone was settled, the tale of Greg, and Bill, and Leonard was recounted once again.

"How are you feeling?" Libby asked.

"I'm fine, really." Lin lifted her mug.

"We're thankful that the killer is behind bars and things can go back to normal." Viv pushed her hair behind her ears.

Libby eyed the young woman with skepticism and then looked to Lin.

"You can speak freely," Lin said. "Viv knows everything."

"And many things I wish I didn't know." Viv frowned.

Libby adjusted in her seat. "What about Sebastian Coffin?"

"I haven't seen him since the night Bill attacked me." A twinge of sorrow grabbed at Lin's heart. She wanted to thank the ghost for alerting her to Bill's attempt to attack from behind. She wondered why he'd disappeared without saying goodbye, or at least a wave of his hand, since he never spoke.

Libby looked crestfallen that the ghost was gone.

"We'd hoped that Coffin might stay around and that perhaps you could learn to communicate with him." Anton stroked his chin.

Lin gave a tiny shrug of her shoulder. She had no idea why ghosts came and went as they did. She glanced across the room to the fireplace. She

J.A Whiting

guessed she wouldn't see Sebastian again and it made her sad. "I guess we'll never figure out what that old key from the leather pouch opens." Lin's voice was tinged with disappointment.

"A key was in the pouch?" Libby asked leaning forward.

"What pouch?" Anton looked confused so Lin relayed the information about the hidden cupboard, the words written under the shelf, and the leather pouch that was found containing a key.

"May I see it?" Libby asked.

Viv went to the kitchen to retrieve the pouch and when she returned to the living room, she handed it to Libby. Libby gently removed the key and turned it over in her hand.

"Can you sense something from holding it?" Lin's tone was hushed.

Libby let out a sigh. "I'd hoped I would." She shrugged and placed the items on the table. "But, nothing."

"*Ours to thee.*" Anton pondered the words. "Certainly seems like whoever left the pouch in the cabinet intended that the key and whatever it opened should go to the person who found it."

Lin told the historian that the "t" on the word "to" looked almost like a fancy "s".

"Ours so thee?" Anton frowned. "That doesn't make any sense."

Viv chuckled. "Maybe it's a puzzle. Lin's always doing word puzzles."

182

Nicky and Queenie sat at attention staring at Lin. Nicky whined.

An idea flashed in Lin's mind. She jumped from her seat. "I need a piece of paper and a pencil."

CHAPTER 24

Everyone in the room watched the young woman with interest as she hurried to the small desk in the corner where she pulled a sheet of paper and a pen from the drawer. She wrote the words from the cupboard on the paper.

"What are you doing?" Viv walked to her cousin's side to look over her shoulder.

Lin was breathless. "*Ours to Thee*. Is it an anagram?" She flipped the letters in her head and wrote new words down. She crossed things out and then let out a yip. "If I change the fancy letter on the word "to" and make it an "s" I can get the word "storehouse." She straightened and grabbed Viv's shoulder. "The storehouse."

Viv blinked.

"Gram called the ell at the back of the house the storehouse."

Viv still looked blank.

"The ell on the back of the house. The 'storehouse.'" Lin's voice shook with excitement. "The ell is original to the house. Sebastian must have hidden something in there. It's in the ell, not in the shed." She took off with the dog and cat chasing her.

Anton and Libby were on their feet and rushed after Lin leaving Viv in the living room looking puzzled. She shook herself, grabbed the old key, and hurried to the back of the house with the others. Lin was already inside the storage space. Over the years, the ell had been used for storing household items and there were suitcases, furniture, Gram's old painting easel, canned goods, old trunks, and odds and ends stacked along the walls and scattered over the floor.

"I guess I need to take this stuff in hand." Viv eyes roved over the mess.

Lin walked around the space crawling over things and pushing boxes out of her way. Queenie and Nicky followed her every move. After several minutes, Lin stepped into a cold current of air and her breath caught in her throat. Moving her feet slowly, she moved around trying to determine the coldest spot. In the far corner, she bent and reached out her hand to touch the old stone partial foundation. Her fingers felt like they'd touched snow and ice. Queenie let out a trill and Nicky howled.

The four people took turns digging in the spot. When it was Viv's turn, she moved the shovel a little to the side and everyone heard the thud of the tool hitting something heavy. After five more minutes of digging, a medium sized chest was pulled from the crevice between the rows of stones and the floor. They all stared at it.

The chest was fashioned of wood, rounded along the sides. Two inch wide metal bands trimmed the edges, and the sides and bottom of the chest were overlaid with thin sheets of metal. Decorative knobs were hammered along the metal edges and a heavy handle was embedded in the top of the chest. A decorative lock held the top lid closed.

Lin nudged her cousin. "Do you have the key? See if it fits."

Viv's hand trembled. "Not me." She pushed the key into Lin's hand. "You figured it out so you should do it."

Lin held the key suspended over the lock for a moment and then she inserted it and turned. It clicked and the lock loosened. Slowly she lifted the lid.

The first thing they saw was a gold chain and pendant resting on top of other items wrapped in linen. With shaking fingers, Lin touched the necklace and took it from the box. "Look." She held it up for the others to see. "There's a tilted horseshoe in the middle of the pendant. Like on Viv's chimney." A white gold upside-down horseshoe was centered on the gold circular pendant.

Libby and Anton leaned closer. Libby's eyes widened and a smile spread over her face. "It was rumored that Emily Witchard Coffin wore such a necklace. This must be hers." She ran her finger over the piece.

"What else is in the chest?" Anton peered inside.

Viv reached in and pushed some of the linen cloth to the side to reveal large leather pouches. She lifted one and handed it to Anton who opened it and tilted the contents into his hand. "Gold Guineas."

The wood and metal chest held five leather folders each one with a piece of artwork inside. Viv inspected one of them. "This looks like a woodcut print."

Anton noticed the monogram signature of the letters "AD" with one letter over the other. He gasped and leaned closer. "These look like the work of Albrecht Dürer."

"Who?" Libby was not familiar with the artist's name.

"He was a famous painter." Viv stared at what the folder held. "He also did woodcut prints and engravings."

"He was one of the most famous artists of the Northern Renaissance," Anton said. Libby removed another pouch. Inside was a golden cross embedded with jewels. They continued to uncover more jewelry and gold coins. The final item was another leather folder containing several papers with hand-drawn maps and cryptograms.

"Are those treasure maps?" Viv's jaw dropped.

Anton couldn't believe his eyes. "You have quite the treasure trove here. You'll need the assistance of an experienced appraiser and a historian familiar with such items."

Viv's face was pale and her hands were shaking.

"My cousin might become a very wealthy woman." Lin grinned and hugged her.

"Oh, no." Viv shook her head. "Sebastian Coffin put these here. He refused to profit from someone else's misfortune and neither will I. If these are authentic pieces then I'll donate everything to a museum or university."

"But, the money." Anton gave Viv a serious look. "It could provide you with things you need, make your life easier."

"I like my life the way it is." Viv smiled at her cousin. "We don't need any more than what we already have." Viv looked at the necklace Lin still held in her hands. "That belongs to you."

Lin was about to protest, but Viv cut her off. "It belonged to a woman who was probably a lot like you." She glanced at Libby for confirmation.

"Yes," Libby nodded. "Information that has been passed down to us from our ancestors tells us that Emily Witchard could see spirits, too."

"Then the necklace is right where it belongs." Viv closed Lin's hand over the pendant and she put her arm over Lin's shoulders. "Just like my cousin is right where she belongs."

Libby grinned. "I couldn't agree more."

Lin's eyes filled with happy tears as the four people and two animals left the storage area. As Lin stepped into the sunshine, a sudden current of cold air engulfed her. She could sense Sebastian Coffin in the breeze.

Thank you for everything.

Lin had a feeling that the ghost wasn't gone after all and that she might be seeing more of him. Very soon.

THANK YOU FOR READING!

BOOKS BY J.A. WHITING CAN BE FOUND HERE:

www.amazon.com/author/jawhiting

To hear about new books and book sales, please sign up for my mailing list at:

www.jawhitingbooks.com

Your email will never be sold, shared, or spammed.

A Haunted Murder

BOOKS BY J. A. WHITING

LIN COFFIN COZY MYSTERIES:

A Haunted Murder (A Lin Coffin Cozy Mystery Book 1)
A Haunted Disappearance (A Lin Coffin Cozy Mystery Book 2) – Soon!
And more to come!

SWEET COVE COZY MYSTERIES

The Sweet Dreams Bake Shop (Sweet Cove Cozy Mystery Book 1)
Murder So Sweet (Sweet Cove Cozy Mystery Book 2)
Sweet Secrets (Sweet Cove Cozy Mystery Book 3)
Sweet Deceit (Sweet Cove Cozy Mystery Book 4)
Sweetness and Light (Sweet Cove Cozy Mystery Book 5)
And more to come!

OLIVIA MILLER MYSTERIES

The Killings (Olivia Miller Mystery Book 1)
Red Julie (Olivia Miller Mystery Book 2)
The Stone of Sadness (Olivia Miller Mystery Book 3)

If you enjoyed the book, please consider leaving a review.

A few words are all that's needed.

It would be very much appreciated.

ABOUT THE AUTHOR

J.A. Whiting lives with her family in New England. Whiting loves reading and writing mystery, suspense and thriller stories.

VISIT ME AT:

www.jawhitingbooks.com

www.facebook.com/jawhitingauthor

www.amazon.com/author/jawhiting

29040680R00126

Made in the USA
Middletown, DE
04 February 2016